NEW YORK REVIEW BOOKS
CLASSICS

WE ALWAYS TREAT
WOMEN TOO WELL

RAYMOND QUENEAU (1903–1976) was born in the French town
of Le Havre and educated at the Sorbonne. He performed his military
service in Morocco. An early association with the Surrealists ended
in 1929, and after completing a scholarly study of literary madmen of
the nineteenth century for which he was unable to find a publisher,
Queneau turned to fiction, writing his first novel, *Le Chiendent*
(published as *Witch Grass* by NYRB Classics), in Greece in the summer
of 1932. Influenced by James Joyce and Lewis Carroll, Queneau sought
to reinvigorate French literature, grown feeble through formalism,
with a strong dose of language as really spoken. He further encouraged
innovation by founding, with the mathematician François Le Lionnais,
the famous group OULIPO (Ouvroir de Littérature Potentielle), which
investigated literary composition based on the application of strict
formal or mathematical procedures (members of the group included
Italo Calvino, Georges Perec, and Harry Mathews). Queneau's many
books, which typically blur the boundaries between fiction, poetry,
and the essay, include *Pierrot mon ami*, *The Sunday of Life*, *Zazie in
the Metro* (made into a movie by Louis Malle), and *Exercises in Style*;
under the name of Sally Mara, he published *We Always Treat Women
Too Well*, a brilliant comic spoof on the excesses of smutty popular
novels. Queneau was the editor of the *Encyclopédie de la Pléiade* as
well as a fine poet, whose lyric "Si tu t'imagines" was a hit for the
celebrated postwar chanteuse Juliette Gréco.

JOHN UPDIKE was born in 1932 in Shillington, Pennsylvania. In
1954 he began to publish in *The New Yorker*, where he continues to
contribute short stories, poems, and criticism. His novels have won
the Pulitzer Prize, among other awards. In 2002 he published the
novel *Seek My Face*.

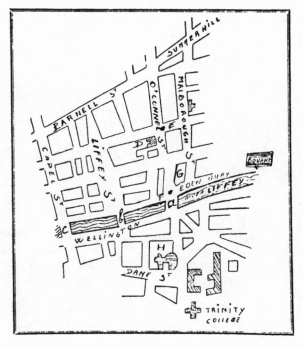

Légende des sigles

st   : street
qu : Quay
b   : Métal bridge
a   : O'Connell bridge
c   : Essex bridge
d   : Hôtel central des Postes
e   : Colonne Nelson (37 m).

f   : statue O'Connell
g   : Académie hibernienne
h   : Collège Green.
La Liffey coule vers l'Est, du côté de Sandymount. Phoenix Park se trouve plus à l'ouest et Kildare st débouche dans Leinster st.

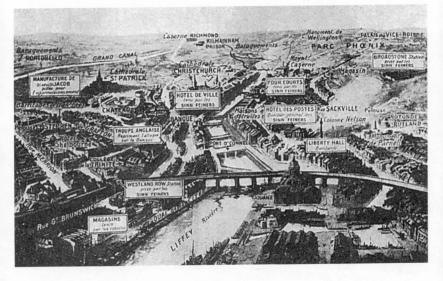

Panoramic View of Dublin

WE ALWAYS TREAT
WOMEN TOO WELL

RAYMOND QUENEAU

(Originally published under the pseudonym Sally Mara)

Translated from the French by
BARBARA WRIGHT

Introduction by
JOHN UPDIKE

NEW YORK REVIEW BOOKS

nyrb

New York

This is a New York Review Book
Published by The New York Review of Books
1755 Broadway, New York, NY 10019

Copyright © 1971 by Editions Gallimard, Paris
Translation copyright © 1981 by Barbara Wright
Foreword copyright © 1981 by Valerie Caton
Introduction copyright © 1983 by John Updike, reprinted from *Hugging the Shore* by John Updike and used by permission of Alfred A. Knopf, a division of Random House, Inc.

Originally published in France as *On est toujours trop bon avec les femmes, par Sally Mara*, 1947 by Editions du Scorpion.

Library of Congress Cataloging-in-Publication Data
Queneau, Raymond, 1903–1976.
 [On est toujours trop bon avec les femmes. English]
 We always treat women too well / Raymond Queneau ; translation by Barbara Wright ; introduction by John Updike.
   p. cm. — (New York Review Books classics) (New york review books classics)
Originally published under the pseudonym Sally Mara.
 ISBN 1-59017-030-X (pbk. : alk. paper)
 I. Wright, Barbara, 1915– II. Title. III. Series. IV. Series: New york review books classics
 PQ2633.U43 O513 2003
 843'.912—dc21

                                    2002011446
ISBN 1-59017-030-X

Book design by Lizzie Scott
Printed in the United States of America on acid-free paper.
10 9 8 7 6 5 4 3 2 1

February 2003
www.nyrb.com

CONTENTS

INTRODUCTION

R AYMOND QUENEAU, that most learned and lighthearted of experimental modernists, in 1947 published, under the pseudonym Sally Mara, a kind of thriller set in Dublin during the uprising of 1916, entitled *On est toujours trop bon avec les femmes*. The book, unlike the American-style novels, sexy and tough, that it burlesqued, did not prove popular with the French public in the Forties; nor has it been popular with the *Queneauistes*. Excluded from the official Gallimard edition of Queneau's oeuvre until 1962, it has been persistently regarded by academics as "an unfortunate but forgivable interlude in a distinguished man's career," we are told by Valerie Caton in her foreword to the belated English translation. She describes as "disturbing" the "flippant and amused manner in which its brutal scenes are presented to the reader," and vouches that the novel's many instances of "deliberate bad taste . . . instead of making the reader laugh, leave him feeling uneasy, even downright appalled." She then cites as an example a passage that did make at least this reader laugh:

> Corny Kelleher had wasted no time in injecting a bullet into his noggin. The dead doorman vomited his brains through an eighth orifice in his head, and fell flat on the floor.

Perhaps *We Always Treat Women Too Well* is less funny in French than in Barbara Wright's frisky, deadpan translation; the borrowing of its Dublin locale and personnel almost entirely from Joyce's *Ulysses* is certainly a less circuitous joke in English than in French, and the risibility of sex and violence may more readily strike American readers hardened by Hammett and Chandler and Spillane than readers saddled with tender Gallic sensibilities. Queneau himself, in a 1944 essay, attacked the greatly successful thriller *No Orchids for Miss Blandish* as glorifying "fascist" behavior at a time when the Western democracies were battling fascists in war. Yet the sado-erotic tradition in French literature has a pedigree going back beyond the notorious Marquis to Rabelais and Villon, and it seems unlikely that the postwar critics who embraced Genet and Georges Bataille would snub Queneau's sportive travesty out of mere squeamishness.

We Always Treat Women Too Well, though sufficiently endowed with Queneau's cerebral prankishness, electric pace, and cut-on-the-bias poetry to give glimmers of delight, is a work of casual ambivalence, wholeheartedly neither parody nor thriller, and with a moral by no means as simple as anti-fascism. A group of Irish Republicans, all named from minor figures in *Ulysses*, storm and take a post office at the corner of Sackville Street and Eden Quay; they kill the doorman and the postmaster, who bears the un-Gaelic name of Théodore Durand and cries "God save the King!" in token resistance. The other workers in the post office are expelled, but one female clerk, Gertie Girdle (close verbal kin to Gerty MacDowell, the limping temptress of Leopold Bloom in the "Nausicaa" episode of *Ulysses*), remains in the lavatory, where she entertains a series of Molly Bloom–like interior monologues until her eventual discovery by the rather bumbling and scatterbrained rebels. Once discovered, she, though at the outset a virgin given to inner raptures over her "beloved fiancé, Commodore Sidney Cartwright," embarks with shameless and inexplicable expertise upon a guerrilla campaign of seduction among her captors, eventually making sexual contact via one orifice or another with six of the seven men. Meanwhile, the British soldiery and a gunboat in the Liffey commanded by Sidney Cartwright besiege the post office and at last recapture it. Yet—and this is the curious fact—no connection between Gertie's seductions and the rebel band's defeat is insisted upon, though it would have been easy for Queneau to make connections, and what little he has of a plot would seem to hinge on them. One of the rebels, Caffrey, is beheaded by a shell while engaged in intercourse; but the hit is a lucky one, from the very erratic gunners of HMS *Furious*, and a quite accidental consequence of his pose. Gertie's sexually active presence among the men functions as a distraction, to be sure, but is never made to appear detrimental to their defense against odds that all come to recognize as hopeless. Cartwright, on the *Furious*, knows that this post office is where his fiancée is employed, and is reluctant, accordingly, to demolish it; so her presence if anything prolongs rather than shortens the lives of the rebels.

Why, then, does this woman, who has no sympathy with the rebellion and "the greatest respect for our gracious King George the Fifth," consort so lustily with her captors? Because, Queneau himself might answer, that's the sort of thing that happens in books like this. In *No Orchids for Miss Blandish*, the heroine is beaten, drugged, and raped at the hands of an armed gang, and falls in love with the ruthless leader. The theme of rape as mutual pleasure is a venerable one, dating back in the West at least to the earthy amours of Zeus. The genre of thriller that Queneau is both protesting and imitating construed sex and violence as parts of a single force-field; it assumed that a tension close to enmity naturally exists between men and women. This was the Thirties and Forties: hard times. "The war between the sexes" was dramatized not only in the cartoons of James Thurber but in the couplings sketched by James M. Cain and Raymond Chandler and *les films noirs*. The apache dance, the grapefruit in the face were acceptable erotic symbols in a world that acknowledged that wooing, like living, had a rough side. Certainly sexual initiation, however considerately cushioned, has the violence of change. For the brides of some tribal societies, the pain and trauma of defloration are diverted from the approved mate onto surrogates; while Gertie Girdle is finding "appeasement of her desires" with her enemies, her proper betrothed on his boat hangs back, reluctant to use his (symbolic) guns because

> this post office conjured up in his mind the engaging personality of his fiancée ... whom he was to (and wished to) marry in the very near future, in order to consummate with her the act that was just a little intimidating to a chaste young man, the strange act whose occult peripeteia transforms a young bint from the virginal state into the pregnant state.

George Bernard Shaw, in his preface to *Man and Superman*, wrote, "If women were as fastidious as men, morally or physically, there would be an end of the race." What Western race better illustrates male reluctance to mate than the Irish? *We Always Treat Women Too Well* is about sexual initiation, and not just Gertie's. The Irish terrorists are portrayed by the mischievous French author as innocent, pious, and primitive; their previous sexual experiences have been with "slatterns harvested on piles of hay or tavern tables still greasy with everything" or with country girls "who get themselves impregnated in the shade of a dolmen or menhir without even so much as letting you get a glance at their nature." Gertie, on the other hand, is dressed in the latest Parisian fashions—a girdle instead of a corset, a brassière, no frilly drawers, and gartered silk stockings. (Queneau is nothing if not fashion-conscious; his novels are shot through with details of clothing to which a surreal intensity of meaning attaches.) The Irishmen are moved to wonder by Gertie's progressive costume:

"No, with her, when you touch her here" (and he took hold of his own torso with both hands), "under her dress, it's skin you're touching, it isn't frills and flounces and whalebone busk, it's skin."

"Is all that true?" asked Dillon.

In a sense, Gertie is the future, bringing death to the past. The Irishmen defend themselves with an antiquated code of honor; doomed to die, they become concerned that in retrospect their heroism will be sullied by their lechery:

"We ought to have killed her right away, but we had to be correct. And in any case, none of this is very important. Except for the cause. For the cause it's bloody annoying if people are going to be able to say we behaved badly in such tragic moments."

The final two survivors, Corny Kelleher and Mat Dillon, concoct an ingenious scheme to achieve Gertie's silence: they do something unspeakable to her. "Now she won't say anything," Kelleher cries, "she won't say anything, and no one will be able to say we weren't heroes, valiant, pure heroes." In the event, the thoroughly violated Gertie lies to her British rescuers, mildly claiming that the Irishmen tried to lift up her skirt to look at her ankles. The horrified British shoot their captives on the spot, but not before Gertie has stuck out her tongue at them and Kelleher has ruefully concluded, "We always treat women too well."

This farce feels genuinely sexy. Queneau has toyed with the forms and codes of hard-boiled fiction without emptying them of content; we are left with an impression of relations between men and women as lawless and predatory. Poor Caffrey, decapitated by a cannon shot in mid-coitus, is likened to "the male of the praying mantis whose upper part has been half-devoured by the female but who perseveres in his copulation." Gertie flees his embrace "covered all over with blood, and moist with a posthumous tribute." In the end, she is sodomized but survives; her assailants are shot. Amid all his cerebration and irony, Queneau hangs tough.

Yet one wonders how many of the few purchasers of *We Always Treat Women Too Well* in its initial edition, by Editions du Scorpion, read it as a straight thriller. From first to last, the style twinkles with Queneau's impudent excesses of precision:

He thumped, rethumped, rerethumped, and rererethumped, his fist down on the tablecloth . . .

The serene night was clasping the dazzling moon in her sooty thighs, and the soft down of her constellations was lightly stirring in the breath of a classic breeze transmitted by the Gulf Stream.

A few moments later Cartwright was standing on his poop deck with a heavy heart, a lumpy throat, an empty stomach, a dry mouth and a glassy eye.

Before he shut the door, Gallager tried to absorb all that beauty in one last look, and closed his eyelids in order not to let the image flee.

A patent spoof on patriotism, murderousness, seductiveness, Irishness, and piety, the novel at bottom makes the deeper satirical point that Queneau's fiction consistently makes: the ineluctable banality of existence, as shown by the subtle clumsiness and foreordained triteness of our attempts to render life into words.

—JOHN UPDIKE

FOREWORD

EVER SINCE it was published in 1947, *We Always Treat Women Too Well* has usually been regarded as a rather odd incursion into the shady world of sado-erotic literature by an otherwise respectable writer. Unlike the rest of Raymond Queneau's novels, issued by the literary publisher Gallimard, it first appeared under the lurid covers of "Editions du Scorpion," in the wake of a whole series of American-style thrillers such as James Hadley Chase's *No Orchids for Miss Blandish*, and Boris Vian's *J'irai cracher sur vos tombes*, both of which enjoyed great success in France in 1946.

Vian's novel was set in the Deep South, and written under the American pseudonym "Vernon Sullivan." Queneau followed suit by publishing *We Always Treat Women Too Well* as the work of a young Irish writer, "Sally Mara," and by giving it an apparently realistic foreign setting—Dublin at the time of the 1916 Easter Uprising. He peppered his novel with Celticisms and Anglicisms, mimicking the thriller novelists' use of transatlantic slang.

Unlike its predecessors, however, *We Always Treat Women Too Well* never caught on as a popular novel. In 1962, Gallimard finally published it under Queneau's own name as part of the ironically entitled *Complete Works of Sally Mara* (in the footnotes to this edition S.M. = Sally Mara) but even then academic critics continued to regard it as a marginal work, an unfortunate but forgivable interlude in a distinguished man's career. The novel rose briefly from obscurity in 1971 when Michel Boisrond decided to make it into a film. He hoped to remain faithful to the spirit of the original but his enterprise failed. The scenes of sex and violence, no longer presented through the prose of a detached narrator, lost all their ambiguity and only added to the novel's dubious reputation.

Obviously, if *We Always Treat Women Too Well* was intended simply as a piece of fantasy writing for popular consumption, then it failed miserably. Yet the truth of the matter is that nothing that Raymond Queneau wrote was ever designed to be taken on one simple level. In his long writing career he produced fifteen novels, from *Le Chiendent* (*The Bark Tree*), published in 1933 when he was thirty, to *Le Vol d'Icare* (*The Flight of Icarus*), which appeared in 1968, eight years before his death on October 25, 1976. Each of the novels reflects the multiplicity of his interests: poetry, mathematics, history, philosophy, language—to mention only the most important. After he became director of the vast Encyclopédie de la Pléiade, Queneau even speculated that his novels might have been placed under subject headings: *Le Chiendent*—phenomenology; *Gueule de Pierre* (1934)—psychology, zoology; *Les Enfants du Limon* (1938)—theology . . . and one could easily take this further; for behind the deceptively straightforward story of a soldier turned shopkeeper in *Le Dimanche de la vie* (1952) (*The Sunday of Life*) lies a subtle meditation on Hegelian philosophy and the nature of Time, whilst the best seller *Zazie dans le métro* (1959) can be read both as a hilarious account of a precocious young girl's first taste of Paris, and a clever attack on the stifling rigidity of standard written French.

Rabelais, in his prologue to *Gargantua* (1535), suggests that readers should approach his writings as a dog would a bone, worrying them constantly in order to extract the precious marrow. Queneau, a great admirer of Rabelais, also demands a conscious effort from his readers. If one reads *We Always Treat Women Too Well* carefully enough, then it emerges, not as an unsuccessful sado-erotic thriller, but as a very cleverly written travesty of that genre. Queneau had no desire to emulate the success of *No Orchids for Miss Blandish*. In fact, he attacked the novel virulently in an article published in the magazine *Front National* in December 1944, based on George Orwell's critical essay "Raffles and Miss Blandish," which had just appeared in the English review *Horizon*. What Queneau found particularly appalling about the success of the gangster thriller was that such literature, which glorified acts of sadism, had been chosen by the very people who were committed to fighting a sadistic Nazi regime. He commented: "That this novel, and others like it, should describe 'fascist' behavior, that these adventures (which, when seen from a political standpoint provoke nothing but horror) should, moreover, be the delight of a democratic public, shows more clearly than anything to what extent literature is remote from life."

In *We Always Treat Women Too Well*, Queneau starts out from a situation strikingly similar to that of Hadley Chase's best seller: an attractive young woman is held hostage by a band of armed men. There follows a series of episodes involving sex and violence culminating in a bloody shoot-out with the authorities in which the men are finally defeated and the woman released. Here, though, the resemblance ends; for the relationship between Gertie and the Irish rebels is quite different from the one which exists between Miss Blandish and her kidnappers.

In Hadley Chase's novel, Miss Blandish is a passive, helpless victim: she is locked up, beaten and drugged by the gang and repeatedly raped by its cold and ruthless leader Slim. When the police finally succeed in releasing her she commits suicide having, despite everything, fallen in love with Slim. As George Orwell points out in his essay, Hadley Chase sets out to make the reader identify with the sadistic acts perpetrated by the gangsters: "In a book like *No Orchids* one is not simply escaping from dull reality into an imaginary world of action. One's escape is essentially into cruelty and sexual perversion. *No Orchids* is aimed at the power instinct."

Compare this with what happens in *We Always Treat Women Too Well*. The novel opens upon a dramatic scene in which a group of IRA men take over the Eden Quay post office in Dublin, murdering or expelling its employees. Yet, no sooner have the men installed themselves, than their campaign begins to founder and they become increasingly unable to control the novel's bloody events. The cause of their downfall is Gertie Girdle, a young post office clerk who happens to be in the "Ladies" when the building is evacuated. By the time the rebels discover her, British troops have besieged the building and the IRA men are reluctantly obliged to keep her prisoner.

At first they are determined to maintain the honor of their cause by being gallant and correct towards their beautiful blonde hostage. Their good intentions soon vanish when Gertie herself changes from an innocent virgin into a ruthless and determined seductress. Siren-like, she draws the men into temptation and to a violent death, gleefully putting her tongue out as the last two rebels face a British firing squad. Gertie is the very opposite of a Miss Blandish, just as her timid and bewildered captors are a mockery of the tough American gangsters. Far from glorifying the power instinct Queneau's novel ridicules it, and the scenes of sex and violence are not titillating but disquieting and absurd.

Perhaps the most disturbing aspect of *We Always Treat Women Too Well* is the flippant and amused manner in which its brutal scenes are presented to the reader. The following description, taken from the opening chapter, in which an English loyalist is shot by the rebels, is typical: "Corny Kelleher had wasted no time in injecting a bullet into his noggin. The dead doorman vomited his brains through an eighth orifice in his head . . ." Here the playfulness of the slang and the preciousness of "an eighth orifice" jar with the violence of the scene itself and with the forcefulness of the verb "vomited." Like the rest of the novel's "humor," these lines are in deliberate bad taste and, instead of making the reader laugh, leave him feeling uneasy, even downright appalled.

In this respect, *We Always Treat Women Too Well* is not only a travesty of a gangster thriller, it is also a travesty of the kind of "black" humor admired by the Surrealists and sometimes wrongly associated with Queneau's work. According to André Breton, black humor liberates the human mind and distances it from everyday reality. By depicting the world in violent and outrageous terms, the black humorist is able to escape from the tedium of bourgeois normality and to enjoy even the most brutal and macabre acts as an entertaining spectacle. In 1940 Breton completed his *Anthology of Black Humor*, which included extracts from Alphonse Allais, Alfred Jarry, Swift, and even the Marquis de Sade. Because of delays to production schedules caused by the war, copies of the book were not released until 1945, and thus its publication immediately preceded that of *No Orchids for Miss Blandish*.

For Queneau, black humor, like the gangster novel, was simply a form of escapism, and its lofty enjoyment of violence and eroticism was yet another glorification of the power instinct. Both kinds of writing constituted, he felt, a dangerous and destructive force within a society which had fought hard to preserve democracy. On November 3, 1945, in one of his regular contributions to *Front National*, he remarked: "Once one has clarified the political nature of fascism, once one has brought out what is specifically Germanic about Hitlerism, there remains nonetheless a certain ideological and practical system which gives to the fascist regime its moral coloring and its philosophical background. Now, this system is not without its links with this or that aspect of the intellectual life of other Western peoples, and notably with the gangster novel and with black humor."

If further proof were needed that *We Always Treat Women*

Too Well was written as a calculated act of literary sabotage, one need only look at the supposed realism of its Irish setting. In the preface to the original edition it was claimed that the novel had been translated from the Irish by a young Frenchman named Michel Presle (Michel Presle = M.P. in the footnotes to this edition) who had met its authoress, Sally Mara, on his visits to Ireland during the 1930s. Yet, although the mention of Eden Quay, the River Liffey, O'Connell Bridge and so on creates a superficial impression of historical and topographical accuracy, Sally Mara's Dublin turns out on closer inspection to be a very literary one indeed. Queneau, in fact, did not describe Dublin from personal experience at all, but instead drew every detail—the names, the places, and even the characters—from the pages of his favorite novelist, James Joyce. Larry O'Rourke, Corny Kelleher, Caffrey and Co. are all out of *Ulysses*; Gertie Girdle's Christian name too is an allusion, appropriately enough, to Gerty MacDowell, the young temptress who catches Leopold Bloom's eye in the "Nausicaa" episode; the rebels' rallying cry is "Finnegans wake!"—and English readers familiar with Joyce's work will undoubtedly find many more parallels.

By presenting his novel in 1947 as a tough new thriller, hot off the popular presses, Queneau deliberately laid a trap for the unwary reader. Anyone looking to Sally Mara's lurid prose to spark off an enjoyable fantasy would soon find himself perplexed. Unable to project into the novel through identification with its characters and yet finding the narrator's flippant bad taste difficult to stomach, he would be thrown back upon the brutality of the events themselves. Small wonder, then, that *We Always Treat Women Too Well* never became a pulp fiction best seller!

This is a startling and ingenious novel. Perhaps it will now have the success it deserves.

—VALERIE CATON, 1981

TRANSLATOR'S NOTES

ABOUT *Ulysses*, Pierre David, a French Queneauphile, has produced a long (and amusing) list of the "correspondences, similarities, analogies, equipollences, coincidences . . . ," etc., between *We Always Treat Women Too Well* and *Ulysses*. (Which he keeps adding to, every year or so.) The attentive reader of this translation will find many words and expressions taken straight from *Ulysses*. He may also find the odd phrase from Synge, here and there.

In all his novels, Queneau delights in innocently introducing bits from French classics into even the most intentionally banal passages. In the "noble" description of the moonlit night in Chapter 23 of the present book, Corneille's "obscure clarity" (of the stars) leads on—via a bit of useful, textbook astronomical information—to Pascal's "ethereal music of the spheres." "Commodore" Cartwright's amazing nautical orders at the beginning of Chapter 31 are a parody of similar orders given in somewhat different circumstances by Alfred Jarry's Ubu Roi. Queneau always approved of my insinuating equally glancing references to English classics into my translations of his books, so don't be surprised when you recognize, apart from Messrs. Joyce and Synge, the odd bits of Shakespeare, Bacon, et al., in this one.

Apart from the subtleties in *We Always Treat Women Too Well* mentioned by Valerie Caton, it seems to me that one of the ironic touches most typical of Queneau is the fact that one gradually comes to realize that Gertie Girdle considers her sometimes surprising activities to be her personal contribution to the War Effort. By subverting the rebels, she is doing her bit for King and Country.

Another fact that I personally appreciate more than somewhat is that the post office at the corner of Eden Quay and Sackville (or O'Connell) Street only ever existed in Raymond Queneau's imagination. For a long time before, during and after the First World War, the building that stood on that spot belonged to Hopkins & Hopkins (the best jewelers in the whole of Dublin's fair city, so I have been authoritatively informed). (See photo in the James Joyce museum in Buck Mulligan's Martello Tower.) Since the departure of Messrs. Hopkins & Hopkins, a few years ago, this corner site has been occupied by . . . The Irish Nationwide Building Society.

—BARBARA WRIGHT, 1981

WE ALWAYS TREAT WOMEN TOO WELL

1

"GOD SAVE the King!" cried the doorman, who had been the manservant of a Lord in Sussex for thirty-six years, but his master had gone down with the *Titanic*, leaving neither heir nor wherewithal to keep up his carssel, as they call it on the other side of St. George's Channel. Back in the country of his Celtic ancestors, the lackey had obtained this modest position in the post office at the corner of Sackville Street and Eden Quay.

"God save the King!" he repeated in a loud voice, for he was loyal to the crown of England.

It was with horror that he had observed the irruption into the post office of seven armed individuals whom he immediately suspected of being Irish Republicans in insurrectionary mood.

"God save the King!" he murmured for the third time.

He did no more than murmur, this time, for he had already manifested his loyalty to such an extent that Corny Kelleher had wasted no time in injecting a bullet into his noggin. The dead doorman vomited his brains through an eighth orifice in his head, and fell flat on the floor.

John MacCormack registered this execution out of the corner of his eye. He didn't consider it absolutely necessary, but this was no time for argument.

The young lady postal clerks were clucking frantically. There were about ten of them, either real English girls or Ulsterwomen, and they in no way approved this turn of events.

3

"Clear these squawking hens out of here!" yelled MacCormack.

So Gallager and Dillon, with both words and gestures, began advising the young ladies to make themselves scarce with all speed. But some of them wanted to go and fetch their waterproofs, and others their handbags; a certain amount of panic became manifest in their conduct.

"Stupid cuntesses!" MacCormack shouted from the top of the stairs. "What're you men waiting for?—clear them out of here!"

Gallager grabbed hold of the first one and gave her bottom a wallop.

"But you must be correct," MacCormack added.

"We'll never manage," muttered Dillon, while being knocked sideways by two damsels charging in the opposite direction.

"Oh! Mr. Dillon!" wailed one of them, as she recognized him.

She stopped short.

"You, Mr. Dillon! Such a respectable man! With a gun in your hand against our King! Instead of finishing my beautiful lace frock!"

Dillon, highly embarrassed, scratched his head. But Gallager came to his aid and, tickling the client under her arms, shouted in her ear:

"Get a spurt on, sappyhead!"

On hearing these words, she fled.

MacCormack rushed up to the first floor, followed by Caffrey and Callinan. When he was out of sight, Gallager caught hold of another girl and caused her hindquarters to reverberate.

"Correct!" he said indignantly. "Correct!"

And, as another posterior was offered to him, he applied his beetle-crusher to it with some force and sent the young person flying—a young person, moreover, who had passed examinations, and correctly answered many questions concerning the geography of the world and the discoveries of Graham Bell.

"Come on, scutter, scutter!" yelled Dillon, full of courage in the face of all this femininity.

The situation was becoming a little clearer, and the feminine personnel were getting a move on, galloping towards the exits, and thence into Sackville Street or Eden Quay.

Two young telegraph clerks were hoping to be expelled like the young ladies, but they had to be content with vulgar biffs on the beezer. They withdrew, disgusted by so much correctitude.

Out in the street, the crowd was gawping at these expulsions. A few shots were heard. The groups began to disperse.

"I think that's the last of them," said Dillon, looking around him.

No more virgins offended his view.

2

On the first floor, the higher-ranking officials didn't make so much fuss. They immediately accepted their expulsion, rushed down the stairs and reached the pavement with all possible speed.

The superintendent was the only one to put up any show of resistance. His name was Théodore Durand, for he was of French origin. But in spite of the sympathy that had always united the French people and the Irish people, the postmaster of the Eden Quay post office had devoted his hearts and souls (he had several, but as we shall soon see this was of no use to him) to the British cause and to the support of the House of Hanover. He regretted the fact that he had neither his tails nor his dinner jacket with him. He had indeed tried to telephone his wife to ask her to bring them, but he lived a long way away, and in any case he didn't have the telephone at home. Hence, he was merely attired in his morning coat. True, he had fought at Khartoum uniformed in shantung and unbleached linen, but even so it disgusted this Frenchman to have to fight these Republicans on behalf of his adopted King with such scant décor-homme.

John MacCormack kicked in the door.

"God save the King!" declared the postmaster, with the heroic resolution of the Unknown Warrior.

He cheesed it presto, though, for John MacCormack had just split his skull with five bloodily and anatomically distributed dumdum bullets.

Caffrey and Callinan shoved the corpse in a corner, and

MacCormack ensconced himself in the postmaster's arm-chair. He manipulated the telephonic apparatus and shouted: "Hallo! Hallo!" into the receiver. At the other end of the line someone answered: "Hallo! Hallo!" So MacCormack pronounced the password:

"Finnegans wake!"

And the someone answered:

"Finnegans wake!"

"MacCormack here. The Eden Quay post office has been occupied."

"Fine. This is the GPO. Everything's going well. The Orange, Green and White flag has been hoisted."

"Hurrah!" said MacCormack.

"Hold on in case there's an attack, though it's unlikely. Everything's going well. Finnegans wake!"

"Finnegans wake!" replied MacCormack.

The someone hung up. And so did he.

Larry O'Rourke came into the office. Very politely, he had positively and practically requested the other high-ranking officials to vamoose. All the employees had been expelled. Dillon, coming from the entrance hall, confirmed this. All they had to do now was await events.

MacCormack lit a pipe, and then offered cigarettes to his pals. Caffrey went downstairs again.

3

ON THE ground floor, Kelleher and Gallager were standing outside the post office, their rifles under their arms. A few onlookers were looking on, at a certain distance. Some sympathizers, at the same distance, were waving their hands, hats or handkerchiefs as a sign of sympathy, and the two rebels answered them from time to time by brandishing their rifles. A few passers-by then started to move off, far from reassured. No Britisher seemed to exist in the vicinity.

Along the quay, a little Norwegian sailing ship was made fast to the sturdy mooring posts, and some Scandinavian seamen were observing these incidents without making any appreciable comment.

Gallager went down the steps to the street and walked the few paces to the corner of Sackville Street. O'Connell Bridge was deserted. On the other side of the bridge, several anxious citizens were stuck like flies round the white marble statue of William Smith O'Brien, awaiting the outcome of the events. After privately saluting the memory of the great conspirator, Gallager turned his back on the Liffey in order to examine the situation in Sackville Street. Facing him, O'Connell's statue, with its fifty bronze figures, had attracted no curious onlookers, in view of its exposed situation; beside it, a tram had come to a standstill, emptied of its passengers and employees. A motionless man stood in front of the statue of Father Matthew. Gallager was less interested in trying to account for the presence of this character than in insulting the memory of the apostle of temperance, which he was in the habit of doing even when he hadn't a drop taken.

The Irish flag was flying over no. 43, the headquarters of the Irish Nationalist Party, it was flying over the Metropole Hotel, it was flying over the GPO. A little farther on, Nelson continued his sojourn in a damp sky, at the top of his 134-foot-high pillar.

Passers-by, bystanders, onlookers, anxious citizens and tourists were becoming scarce. From time to time a rebel or some rebels ran across the street, rifle or revolver in hand.

Still no reaction from the British.

Gallager smiled and went back to his post.

"Everything all right?" asked Kelleher.

"The flag of Eire is flying over the most important roofs in O'Connell Street," replied Gallager.

Naturally, he never said Sackville Street.

"Finnegans wake!" they shouted in chorus, waving their rifles over their heads.

A few sympathizers replied, but some onlookers withdrew.

Caffrey began to close the windows.

4

ALL THE same, said Gertie Girdle to herself, all the same, these modern lavatories are still not perfect, this flushing system makes such a noise, goodness gracious! a noise like a riot, not that I've ever heard a riot but I've sometimes heard a rabble, a rabble brawling and babbling, this flushing system makes a noise like that, it bawls, and it's still bawling, that gurgling noise the tank makes as it fills up again, it's never-ending, it's definitely not perfect yet, it lacks discretion. I must tidy my hair a bit. To please whom, I wonder. My beloved fiancé, Commodore Sidney Cartwright, hasn't arrived yet to admire my beautiful mane. When shall I see my beloved fiancé again? When? And until then, my goodness gracious, whom shall I be able to please? Those people running, I wonder why. But my goodness gracious, those people running. I wasn't thinking about them. I was thinking about my hair. That's a good two minutes there've been those sounds of feet, of running, of stamping feet. Just now. At the same time as the flushing system, there was something like a ... Something like a what ... A shot. It's ridiculous. A suicide. Perhaps Monsieur Durand has committed suicide. He loves me so much. And so respectfully. I don't love him. There, my hair's more or less all right now. A shot. He's killed himself for love of me. It's stupid. And those people who never stop running. They must have gone mad. Goodness gracious. How stupid I am. Goodness gracious, goodness gracious. That's what it is, there's a fire. A fire. Why don't they shout "Fire!" if there's a fire? They aren't shouting "Fire!" It's this flushing system that's given me incendiary ideas. Even so it's high time I came out of here. Mrs. Kane will say I've been away too long again. What a job. Ah, all the same they've stopped running. All the same. What a job. Mrs. Kane with her grey hair with its pink dandruff. I've never seen a riot, or a revolution. They're talking about one here. They're talking about one. They're talking about one. The war in France means peace for here. Isn't it peaceful. Isn't it quiet. They've stopped running. But why have they stopped running. Stopped. Stopped. Everything's stopped. It's time I went out of here. Then why don't I go out? Don't I go out? Don't I go out? Why not? There. I've done everything I had to do here. And now this silence. Put my hand on that protective bolt. Slide the bolt. Open the door gently. Why gently? Why all these precautions? My goodness gracious, am I going mad? It's stupid. I'll open the door.

5

HAVING pushed the door open she perceived, in the corridor, a man with a revolver in his hand. He didn't see her. She quickly pulled the door shut again and, leaning against the wash-basin, pressed both her hands to her heart, which had started beating so hard it was nearly breaking her ribs.

6

"I'VE BEEN the rounds," said Larry O'Rourke. "Not a soul. Caffrey, Kelleher and Gallager have locked everything up downstairs, except the main door. They're ready to barricade it if need be."

"No danger," said Dillon.

"Meaning?" asked MacCormack.

"That they won't need to barricade it."

"You think there won't be any English reaction?"

"No. They've got other things to do. It's in the bag."

"Meaning?" asked MacCormack.

"That they'll capitulate without firing a single shot."

"Monkeydoodle," said MacCormack.

O'Rourke shrugged his shoulders.

"No point in arguing. We shall see. We must obey orders."

"For the moment, there's no problem," said Dillon. "All we have to do is wait."

"Well then, let's wait," said O'Rourke.

MacCormack pointed to the corpse of Théodore Durand, late of the Civil Service.

"We aren't going to leave it to ferment here."

"It won't have time," retorted Dillon. "This very evening we'll give it back to the British and they'll bury it. Just like that. A little present before they leave."

"We could put it in another room," said MacCormack.

He looked at the stiff in disgust, even though it was his own work, after all.

"O'Rourke can cut it up," said Dillon, "and we'll take it away in little bits and chuck it down the lavatory."

MacCormack banged his fist down on the table and a few drops of ink spurted out of the ink-well.

"In the name of God! Kindly show some respect for the dead!"

"And in any case, he's got the wrong idea about the study of medicine," said O'Rourke, who was in his last year.

"Then you don't by any chance cut up corpses?"

"This is no time for such arguments," said MacCormack.

"We've got plenty of time," Dillon retorted. "While we're waiting for the British to surrender, we've got plenty of time to argue. Tell me, Larry O'Rourke, in what way have I got the wrong idea about the study of medicine when I maintain that you would be capable of cutting a civil servant up into little pieces? And I may add, Larry O'Rourke, that you have plenty of time to talk, and we might just as well talk about that as about anything else, because we shan't have a great deal to do until we hear that the British are leaving Dublin for their inclement, Zeppelin-studded skies."

"This is a solemn hour, Dillon," said MacCormack. "It isn't the moment to give way to smug optimism."

"Well said," said O'Rourke.

"You'll see, you'll see, the British . . ."

"Dillon, I'm in charge here. Shut up."

MacCormack was highly embarrassed at having had to cause discipline, the strength of insurrections, to reign, and he started fiddling with a stick of sealing-wax. Callinan, his hands in his pockets, slumped back in an armchair, was looking for flies on the ceiling to spit at, but it was rather high. O'Rourke, at the window, was looking at the deserted quay, and at O'Connell Bridge where the passers-by were becoming scarcer and scarcer. The only activity he could observe was that of the Norwegian sailing ship which was feverishly fitting out. This displeased him. He turned back to

MacCormack. The latter, mechanically adorning his face with a moustache by squeezing the stick of sealing-wax between his lip and nose, said in a colorless voice to Callinan:

"Move the civil servant into the next room. Dillon can help you."

They did so.

7

ALL THE same, I'm not going to stay here until the end of my days, said Gertie to herself. Goodness gracious, it was bandits, Republicans, looting the post office. They must be gone by now. But it rather seems to me that they aren't gone. It's the others who're gone. The Others: us. There really was a shot. Then it must be a riot. Their Revolution. And that man with the revolver, a Republican. An Irish Republican. My goodness gracious! God save the King! And here I am, alone, in their hands. Almost in their hands, because there's still this lavatory door separating me from them, protecting me from them. A door. A door can be broken down. And when they've broken it down, then I shall be in their hands. Alone. Alone. How many are they? Still this silence. But they won't break this door down. Of course not. Of course not. They won't dare. This is the LADIES' lavatory. Ha ha ha. And I shall stay locked in here until the British come and rescue me. Unless they have a woman with them. A woman who will inevitably come here, who'll try to open the door. And . . . And . . . They'll break down the door. They'll break down the door.

8

AFTER they'd deposited the doorman's corpse in a small empty office, Gallager and Kelleher went to join Caffrey, who was still on guard duty at the door opening on to Eden Quay. Onlookers and sympathizers had disappeared. A cyclist crossed O'Connell Bridge; he was wearing a top hat and a frock coat; he must have been about twenty-five. When he got to the O'Connell statue he turned round and went back in the direction of Trinity College.

"It's quiet," said Gallager.

"Very," replied Caffrey.

Kelleher brought out a packet of cigarettes and they began to smoke, leaning on their rifles.

In front of them, the Norwegian sailing ship had nearly finished fitting out. They could see the captain coming and going and the first officer directing operations.

"The Vikings are slinging their hook," said Caffrey. "They're in a funk."

"They're quite right," said Gallager. "Let them go, and take the Angles and other Saxons with them."

Meanwhile the sailors had let go the ropes and the little sailing ship was departing, descending the Liffey towards the sea. The three rebels waved them goodbye. The Scandinavians replied.

"Have a good trip," shouted Kelleher. "Have a good trip."

The little sailing ship was going well. Soon it came to the bend in the river and disappeared. The three men remained silent. They finished their cigarettes at the same time.

"Funny sort of rising," sighed Caffrey. "Funny sort of rising. I never imagined it would be so simple."

"You think it's all over, then?" Gallager asked him.

"Don't *you?*"

Gallager and Kelleher burst out laughing.

"Do you really think the British will go away just like that?"

"They have slow reactions, in any case."

"Very likely."

"And then, what with their other war on their hands, maybe they'll just give up, now they've seen our strength."

His discourse was interrupted by the sudden arrival of an open car, sporting the Orange, Green and White flag, which ground to a halt in front of them. A chap jumped out of the car and ran over to them.

"Finnegans wake!" he shouted.

"Finnegans wake!" the three men shouted back, nevertheless manifesting the first signs of an aggressive retreat.

"Are you occupying this building?" the chap demanded authoritatively.

"Yes."

"How many are you?"

"Seven. You can come and see our Commander-in-Chief. John MacCormack."

But the latter, alerted by O'Rourke, had appeared at the window.

"Finnegans wake!" he shouted.

"Finnegans wake!" the chap replied. "Are you the chief?"

"Yes."

"What have you got in the way of weapons?"

"Our rifles. Some revolvers."

"Ammunition?"

"In our pockets."

"Provisions?"

"None."

"Right. Come down. I'll give you a machine-gun, some boxes of ammunition, and some provisions."

"Are we going to have to hold out against a siege?" asked Caffrey.

"Maybe. Come down."

Caffrey stayed by the door. Gallager and Kelleher started humping the utensil and the boxes. Dillon and Callinan watched them with interest.

"Can you see where to put your machine-gun?" asked the chap.

"Yes," replied MacCormack.

But the chap wasn't convinced.

"You enfilade the bridge. From that window there, on the ground floor."

9

A CAR'S stopped. Perhaps they've come to fetch them. Or perhaps they're leaving. Who are they. How many are they. Maybe I know some of them. Or one of them. One all the same. Out of all the men I've seen here, in Dublin, in this Eden Quay post office, there must have been *some* Republicans. I shall probably recognize *one* of them. No. There aren't any women with them. That's certain. If there was one, she'd already have come here. And when I do recognize that one Republican, where will that get me? It could well be one who hates me. One I might have kept waiting a bit too long on the other side of the counter. One I might have made write the address again because he didn't know much English. A chap from Connemara. And to think that some of them want to go back to speaking Irish. As if Sir Théodore Durand were to go back to speaking French. What has become of Sir Théodore. Maybe they've taken him prisoner. Or killed him. Maybe that shot was for him. Poor Sir Théodore, who loved me so much and so respectfully. But maybe he escaped. Maybe he was one of the people I heard running. Maybe *his* footsteps were amongst those I heard. Such a dignified man. Maybe he had to run. Ha ha ha. Him, run. Ha ha ha. So dignified, who loved me so much. And me still locked in here.

10

"THAT'S the right place for it," said the chap. "Will your men know how to use it?"

"Of course," said MacCormack, who had come downstairs to talk to the strategist.

They said farewell and the car drove off.

"Well, are you pleased with it?" asked MacCormack.

They looked at the boxes of ammunition and provisions.

"Looks promising," said Kelleher.

"Just as well," said Gallager.

"There's nothing to drink," said Caffrey.

"By the way," said MacCormack, "what about the chap you knocked off?"

"We put him in a little office."

"And yours?" asked Caffrey.

"Also in a little office."

"If there's going to be a barney," said Kelleher, "we ought to get rid of them."

"That's just what I think," said MacCormack.

"All we have to do is chuck them in the Liffey," said Gallager.

"That wouldn't be correct," said MacCormack.

"Supposing," said Gallager, "that the British take it into their heads to counter-attack and we have to hold out here for, I don't know, a little while."

"That's only suppositions," said Caffrey.

"Well," Gallager went on, "it wouldn't be very clever to stay here with a couple of corpses on our hands. We could toss them into the art school garden. The Hibernian Academy is right behind us."

"All he ever thinks of is getting shut of the corpses," said MacCormack.

"Let them stay where they are!" exclaimed Caffrey. "In any case, this isn't going to drag on for days on end."

"There's something in what he says," said Kelleher.

"Why don't we talk about drink," Caffrey went on. "There's a great shortage of it. If we had a hard time, we'd feel a hell of a need for it."

"There's something in what he says," said Kelleher.

"That's true," said MacCormack. "Well, two of you go and fetch a case of uisce beatha and two or three of Guinness from the first pub you see in O'Connell Street."

"Where are we going to get the rhino for whiskey and Guinness?" asked Caffrey.

"You can write out a requisition indent."

"All we have to do is take the cash from here," said Caffrey.

"That wouldn't be correct," said MacCormack.

"That's right," said Kelleher, "all we have to do is make out an indent."

MacCormack called Dillon and Callinan to come and re-place Caffrey and Kelleher during their expedition.

Dillon and Callinan admired the machine-gun.

11

CAFFREY and Kelleher pushed open the swing door of the pub.

"Hoopsa!" they called out, for there was no one there.

Some half-empty glasses of Guinness were turning sour on tables that no vigilant dish cloth had so far bedaubed. Two or three stools had been knocked over by hasty departures.

"Hoopsa!" called Caffrey and Kelleher.

A man gradually began to surface from behind the counter. He looked in no way reassured. A slick of hair was plastered down over his forehead, and he had a little Austrian corporal's moustache.

"Finnegans wake!" shouted Kelleher and Caffrey.

"What did you say?" asked the innkeeper.

"Finnegans wake!" yelled the two insurgents.

"Oh, personally," said Smith (for such was the innkeeper's name), "oh, personally, I don't go in for politics. And God save the King!" he added, spurred on by his foolish fear.

"Shall we knock him off?" suggested Caffrey.

"The chief told us to be correct," retorted Kelleher.

He picked up a bottle of Guinness and broke it over the skull of Innkeeper Smith, whose head began to exude stout-grenadine. But he wasn't dead, merely a little roughed-up.

"Give us a case of uisce beatha," said Caffrey, "and ten cases of Guinness."

"We're going to give you an indent," added Kelleher.

Smith, propping himself up against the counter with both

hands, still stunned, watched, with a hazy eye, the stout-grenadine spreading out over his mahogany counter.

"Come on," said Caffrey, "are you going to get a move on, perfidious publican?"

He thumped him.

The other lashed out slightly, in a sudden burst of vitality, and then collapsed in a swoon, pissing blood out of all the vessels in his skull.

"We'll manage without him," said Kelleher. "But you might just as well write out the indent."

"You do it," said Caffrey. "I'll go and look for a wheel-barrow."

"Why not you?"

"Me what?"

"Write the indent."

Caffrey scratched his head.

"No, not me."

"Why not you?"

Caffrey scratched his head.

"Leave me be."

"That's no reason," said Kelleher.

The pool of blood was spreading round the innkeeper's head, and it was so deep that Caffrey could see his face reflected in it as in a mirror. Which stimulated him to candor.

"There *is* a reason," said Caffrey.

"What is it? We're wasting time."

"I can't write."

Kelleher looked him up and down. They came from different groups and hardly knew each other. After this examination, Caffrey heard himself first addressed as follows:

"What a disaster!"

And then: "Should have said so before. Right, you go and find a wheelbarrow, and I'll make out the indent."

Caffrey looked at the innkeeper who was flat out, not

breathing through his nose; even his blood wasn't pissing out any more.

"Do you think he's defunct?"

"Go and fetch the wheelbarrow," said Kelleher.

12

ALL THE same, I'm not going to stay on my feet for hours on end, said Gertie to herself, looking at her wrist-watch, which she didn't know was an invention of Blaise Pascal. Two and a half hours I've been here. It's exhausting. I'm tired, tired, tired. All the same, I'm not going to stay on my feet for hours on end. The rebels have been making a great commotion all this time. They've been going up and down stairs. They seemed to be carrying some heavy things, goodness gracious, perhaps they're going to blow up the post office. I must escape. I must escape. No. They aren't going to blow up the post office. But all the same I'm not going to stay on my feet for hours on end. All the same, I'm not going to sit down on that seat, either. How awful. Those Republicans. That's what they can reduce one of His Britannic Majesty's subjects to. The Huns must be behind it somehow. All the same, I'm not going to sit down on that seat. How infamous. How humiliating. But I'm so tired, so tired. No, my goodness gracious, I'm not going to, I'm not going to. Unless I had a reason to. Unless it was legitimate. If, for instance. If, for instance. Yes. Then I could sit down. And rest. I'm so tired, so tired.

13

THE CASES of uisce beatha, and Guinness, and ammunition belts, were carefully tidied away in disorder in a room next to the little office which was the temporary residence of the two corpses of the British civil servants mown down in the cause of the insurrection.

"It's quiet," said MacCormack, and he went back up to the first floor.

Kelleher was dreaming by the machine-gun. Gallager and Caffrey, sitting on the steps, their rifles between their legs, were chatting.

"In the island where I was born," said Gallager, "which is called Inniskea, we like storms and tempests on account of the shipwrecks. After, we comb the beaches and pick up whatever we can. We find a bit of everything. We live well in our little Isle of Inniskea."

"Why did you leave it?" asked Caffrey.

"To come and fight the English. But when Ireland has been freed, I shall go back to Inniskea."

"You'd do better to go back straightaway," said Caffrey. "You'd find plenty of wrecks there."

"So I should hope. We have a special stone for that, in our village."

"A stone?"

"Yes. It's wrapped up in flannel, like a babe-in-arms. Sometimes, when it's been fine for a long time and we're dying of starvation, when there's nothing left, then we bring out the stone, we walk it all round the island, but especially over by the cliffs, and it never fails, the sky turns black, the boats get lost, and the next day we're collecting the debris, everything, tins of food, astrolabes, great big whole gruyères, slide rules . . ."

"I shouldn't really say it," Caffrey commented, "but even so, we're a bit backward in our island, and you're even more so in yours. Luckily, we're going to change all that."

"Backward—what d'you mean by that?"

"There's no country left in the world where they still worship stones. Except where the savages live, the pagans in Australia and Mexico."

"Are you by any chance insinuating that I'm a savage?"

"No, of course not," said Caffrey. "Hey, look at that squaw."

A young woman was crossing O'Connell Bridge, with a determined gait.

"She's fubsy," observed Gallager, who had the keen eye-sight of all the natives of the Isle of Inniskea.

"She's courageous," observed Caffrey, who was capable of appreciating this quality in other people, even though he had no inner criterion on which to base a sound judgment.

The young woman had reached the corner of Eden Quay.

"She's pretty," said Gallager. "I rather think I know her."

"It's us she's after," said Caffrey. "Personally, I like them a bit taller."

She crossed the road and stopped outside the post office door. She did blush, though.

"Well, my miss," said Gallager, "this is no day to be going for a walk. Dublin's in a state of chassis, you know."

"I do indeed, mister," replied the girl, lowering her eyes. "I've already had some experience of it."

"Have you had trouble?"

"Don't you remember?"

"I rather think I know you, but *I've* never caused anyone any trouble."

"Have you already forgotten? You . . . you . . . you kicked me."

"You see," said Caffrey, "you weren't correct."

"Were you one of the young ladies in the post office?"

In his confusion, Gallager hid the tip of his nose in the barrel of his rifle.

"I've come back to fetch my handbag which I lost because of you, you big brute."

"You could go and fetch it," said Caffrey.

"Nothing doing!" replied Gallager.

"You aren't very gallant," said Caffrey.

"We've got other things to do," said Gallager.

"All the same, the British are miles away," said Caffrey.

"Have you really not seen my bag?" asked the shawl. "It's green, with a gold strap, and it contains one pound, two shillings and six pence."

"I haven't seen that," said Gallager.

He felt like either kicking or slapping her posterior, according to the way his inspiration took him. But Caffrey seemed to have some pretentions to that famous correctitude advocated by MacCormack, a correctitude which even bordered on the gallant.

"I'll go and look," says he.

"Forget it," said Gallager.

Kelleher came to the door.

"What's up?" he asked anxiously.

"She's lost her handbag," said Gallager.

"She's fubsy," said Kelleher approvingly.

"Oh!" said the young lady postal clerk, blushing.

"Seeing that you're both here," said Caffrey, "I'll go and see whether I can't find her bag."

"Oh!" said the young lady postal clerk, reverting to sugared-almond pink. "How kind of you!"

"All the same," said Gallager, "we *have* got other things to do."

14

ALL THE same, now I've finished, I can't go on sitting on this seat forever. Fatigue has its bounds. Fatigue has its limits. Courage. Courage. I must be courageous. Like a true English girl. A subject of the British Empire. Oh God, oh my King, I must be energetic. I'll stand up. I'll pull the chain. No. I won't pull the chain. It'll make a noise. Attract their attention. Energy is not imprudence. There is a definite difference between the two. According to the logic of John Stuart Mill, at any rate. Definitely. Probably. But it isn't clean not to pull the chain after using the ... Yes. No. Indeed. It isn't clean. It isn't hygienic. It isn't British. But I have a feeling they're there. I seem to hear them talking. The brutes. The rebels. Would they even know what the sound of flushing water means, if they heard it. They wouldn't. They must all come from the slums where there isn't any hygiene. Maybe some of them even come from the Aran Islands or the Blaskets, where they don't speak English, where they persevere with their Celtic jargon and don't know anything about the lavatories of our modern, imperial civilization, and even, and even, there may be some who come from the Isle of Inniskea where, so I've been told, they worship a stone wrapped up in wool, instead of worshiping Saint George and the God of the Armies. There are only two things they can make, there: the men make Guinness, and the women make guipure, Irish raised point lace. But it's going out of fashion. Why didn't I go to France instead, to Paris, for example?

They've no idea how to dress, here. *I* know something about the latest fashion, though. But the women here, Irish raised point lace is as far as they go.

15

"WHAT THE hell's that stupid goose doing there?" asked Larry O'Rourke.

The three others jumped, and the young lady postal clerk blushed scarlet.

"No, but what the hell is she doing there?" Larry O'Rourke repeated. "You aren't here to dally with fair Vestals. Even though," he added, having given this person the once-over, "she isn't one."

"She isn't a what?" asked Gallager.

"Oh!" said the person in question, who had understood because, as we have mentioned, she had passed examinations, and even studied the works of William Shakespeare.

"Who are you?" inquired Larry O'Rourke.

"She's come to fetch her bag," said Gallager.

"I was just going to fetch it for her," said Caffrey.

"You've got other things to do, especially as there's trouble brewing. They've just phoned from the GPO that the British are beginning to wake up."

"They won't do anything," said Caffrey.

"Young lady," said Larry O'Rourke, "you'd do better to stay at home, whatever happens."

"At least you finally addressed me as 'Young lady.' And not before it was time."

"Caffrey, go and fetch her bag, so she can vamoose and leave us in peace."

"Couldn't I go and fetch it myself?"

"No. We don't want any women here."

"I'll go," said Caffrey.

The young lady postal clerk didn't move. She looked at the three men, marveling at their extravagance, their actions, and their perverse penchant for firearms. She was a small brunette, with a moderately frolicsome air, of a rather fleshly and architectural build, but dressed with modesty. Her face was adorned with nostrils tiptilted towards the skies, and, all things considered, there may have been something Spanish about her.

However that may have been, having been hit in the belly by some lead, she collapsed, dead and bleeding.

The British were appearing on all sides. They'd taken their time to get going, but now they were here-they-coming, handling more or less automatic weapons, rushing up from right and left, bringing the rebels within their more or less approximative line of sight.

Kelleher, Gallager and Larry O'Rourke jumped back three paces presto and slammed the door shut. Kelleher pounced on the Maxim and started spraying Bachelor's Walk with its oh! how murd'rous bullets. Other rebel weapons, situated elsewhere, started to pepper O'Connell Bridge, even though there was no one to be seen on it. All over the place bits of granite or asphalt started flying from the surface of parapets, mooring posts or pavements. A few British fell here and there. They were very soon removed, because their medical corps was equal to its task.

The young lady postal clerk was lying on the ground, quite destroyed. She had fallen on her back with her legs sprawling. She was wearing black cotton stockings. Her skirt had got caught up. A light sea-breeze caused a frou-frou among her frou-frous. Above the black cotton stockings, a little human flesh could be perceived. From her transpierced belly her rather reddish blood was flowing. The puddle grew around this body which was arguably virginal, and certainly desirable, at least to the great majority of normal men.

Gallager took up his position at a window and shouldered his rifle. To one side of his line of sight, on the left, he could see the poor young lady, and her legs. He felt in his pocket for some ammunition. There he encountered a certain stiffening of his being. And while his rifle oscillated vaguely and ineffectually, he sighed. Thus several Britons managed to approach O'Connell Bridge.

16

ON HEARING the first shots, Callinan and Dillon flattened themselves against the wall. MacCormack, the courageous chief, stood up. Revolver in hand, taking no precautions, he went and looked out of the window.

"They're at the corner of Ormond Quay and Liffey Street."

"Many of them?" asked Dillon.

"They're taking cover. Like you."

MacCormack took aim at a Briton who was galloping from one pile of wood to another. Timber that had come from Norway. But he didn't shoot.

"It wouldn't do any good."

When they had got their breath back, Dillon and Callinan went and fetched their rifles and took up their positions at different windows. Below them they heard Kelleher's machine-gun firing two or three bursts.

"It works," said Callinan, with satisfaction.

"There are some more of them coming from Crampton Quay and Aston Quay," said MacCormack.

A bullet whistled past his ear, but as he was very courageous he merely leant a little farther out of the window.

"Well well," he said, "a bird's got the chop."

He had just caught sight of the body of the young lady postal clerk.

"How did she get herself killed?" he murmured. "Poor little thing. Her dress has got rather caught up. That would have made her blush when she was alive. It isn't correct."

The other two, in a fit of daring, forgot the menacing aerial lead of the British weaponry and took a squint at the corpsified bird. From where they were they didn't find it very interesting, so they went back to their shooting.

17

ALL THE same, said Gallager to himself, wiping his viscid hand down the leg of his pants, what I've just done isn't very pretty. And then, it might bring bad cess to me. O Virgin Mary, pray for me! O Virgin Mary, you understand, it was the emotion.

A bullet ricochetted near him.

He got his gun back into position, shut his eyes and started shooting at random.

18

Caffrey discovered the young lady's handbag at the same time as his lack of enthusiasm for battle. An unskilled worker at Guinness's Brewery, his attitude towards the King of the English had always been one of disgust. It was his very specific antipathy towards the Anglo-Saxon and Hanoverian throne that had incited him to get involved in this rebellion, which was a real bugger. Insurrection was no joke. There was a hell of a racket. He could hear stone cracking and bullets flying. He put the bag down on the money order desk and stood there, whitish and fairly immobile.

He was having great trouble with his bowels.

All of a sudden.

And he was ashamed. Being somewhat uneducated, not to say illiterate, he was unaware that such a thing had happened before to the most indisputably courageous of men. He wanted to liquidate this question immediately, and brought his hands up to his braces, which were emerald green. But he was ashamed. Once again.

He remembered John MacCormack's orders, and the necessity of being correct.

Even though his memory had been slightly shaken by the recent events, he remembered that in the corridor, to the left of the stairs, there were two doors of a quite different aspect from those that opened on to the offices. He had noticed them in passing, while chasing out the laggards during the occupation of the building. And he thought that those doors had a more or less certain connection with his present needs.

Bowing to MacCormack's clearly expressed desire that they should leave the Eden Quay post office as clean when they left it as it had been when they entered it, Caffrey, holding his stomach with one hand, stumbled, greenish, towards the corridor to the left of the stairs.

He was sweating.

In a relatively short time he reached the first of these doors. LADIES was the word written on it in relief. But Caffrey couldn't read, not even in Irish. And even less in English, a particularly complicated tongue. Those six letters seemed to him to be the magic indication of his conquest of courage. He turned the handle but didn't open the door. He turned it the other way and the door didn't open. He reverted to the first rotational direction and the door didn't open. Rotation in the opposite direction didn't open the door. He pulled the bloody door. He pushed it. It didn't move in any direction. Then he realized that it was shut. This saddened him at first, because of the great urge he felt to enter this place, but then, since at this very exact moment and at this very precise spot on the inhabited earth, he was, *hic et nunc*, playing the part of a rebel, he began to reflect on the present situation.

The Irish mind, as we know, does not obey the rules of Cartesian logic, any more than it obeys those of experimental method. Neither French nor English, but fairly close to Breton, it proceeds by "intuition."

As Caffrey couldn't open the door, he therefore had the *ankou*[1] that someone was locked in behind it. This *anschauung*[2] immediately tied his guts up in a knot. Wiping away the

---

1. Celticism for "intuition." M.P.

2. Germanism for *ankou.* M.P.

sweat that was trickling down his puss, he forgot his egocentric troubles and, discovering his duty *d'un seul coup d'un seul*,[3] he decided to inform MacCormack of the discovery he had just made.

---

3. Gallicism for *anschauung*. M.P. (Also gallicism for the Anglo-Saxon cliché "in the twinkling of an eye." B.W.)

19

IN THE middle of the fusillade, Gertrude heard a step approaching, a man's hesitating step. Maybe he was wounded. She could tell that he was leaning against the door. She saw the handle turn to the left, then to the right, then to the left, then to the right. She perceived the pressure of the body trying to force the door open. Then there was silence. Next, in the middle of the fusillade, she heard the step moving away. But it was a decided step, now. The heels sounded confident.

During the whole of this time she had been thinking of nothing. Absolutely nothing.

Next, she reflected, in fragmentary fashion, on what was going to happen. She was at a loss for elements to nourish her fear. Therefore, what she was experiencing wasn't exactly fear. Not precisely fear. She was aware that the near future would go far beyond her imagination.

Automatically, she opened her bag and took out her comb. She wore her hair short, which was still a rarity in Dublin, a new fashion. Examining herself in the mirror over the washbasin, she liked the look of herself. And considered herself dangerously beautiful. She ran her comb through her hair, slowly, deliberately. The slight scraping of its tortoiseshell teeth over her cranial skin, followed by the gentle undulation of her curls, made her quiver most delightfully. She stared at her eyes, as if she were trying to hypnotize herself.

There was no more time, and the fusillade had stopped.

20

THE FUSILLADE had stopped. The British, having discovered the positions occupied by the rebels, were now engaged in consultations of a tactical and strategic nature. They had taken cover all along the right bank of the Liffey. On the left bank, they had advanced no farther than Capel Street on the left, and the Old Dock footbridge on the right. In Sackville Street, nothing seemed to be happening.

MacCormack, aided by Callinan and O'Rourke, was taking advantage of this lull to barricade the windows. Dillon went downstairs to fetch a case of ammunition. He passed Caffrey, who was courageously marching up the stairs.

"Everything all right down there?" he asked, as he went by.

"Hrm," grunted Caffrey.

"Something wrong?"

"No, no."

MacCormack was blocking up the interstices of a shutter with Théodore Durand's files. He was a firm believer in the efficacity of many thicknesses of paper as a protection against bullets, and in any case he didn't like bureaucracy. He was feeling happy.

He was irritated, therefore, to hear himself being disturbed in this pleasant and exciting task.

"Chief," said Caffrey.

"What?"

"Chief."

"What is it?"

"Chief."

MacCormack turned round.

"Everything all right downstairs?"

"Yes."

"Good."

"Not altogether."

"What?"

"It's . . ."

"Get a spurt on."

"Downstairs . . ."

"Well?"

"In the bog . . ."

"What?"

"Someone."

"Well?"

"Not one of us."

MacCormack was a leader of men, therefore, by his very nature as a leader of men, he caught on immediately.

"A Britisher?" he asked.

"Prolly," replied Caffrey.

Thinking even more cogently, MacCormack asked:

"Did you lock him in?"

"He'd locked himself in."

"But outside the door . . ."

"What?"

"No one?"

"No. I rushed upstairs to tell you."

"He'll vamoose," said MacCormack.

Caffrey scratched his head.

"Didn't think of that," he said.

He added:

"It took me by surprise. Just like that. Locked in the bog. Can't think of everything. I rushed upstairs to tell you."

Larry O'Rourke and Callinan had begun to listen.

"What's he blethering about?" asked Callinan.

"What is he saying?" questioned O'Rourke.

"A Britisher in the lavatory," said MacCormack.

"I thought you'd evacuated all the rooms," said O'Rourke, "and that you'd made sure there was no one left."

"Yes," said MacCormack, who'd forgotten that O'Rourke had made himself personally responsible for this verification.

He still didn't have quite all it takes to be a leader of men. He didn't know how to bawl people out. Larry O'Rourke, who was educated, showed, on the contrary, great talent as a sub-leader. And then, he was a methodical thinker.

"The bog!" exclaimed Caffrey. "What an idea—to hide there!"

"We must anticipate all our opponents' ideas," said O'Rourke.

MacCormack made an effort, and recovered his intellectual rank as leader.

"But," he asked Caffrey, "how did you find out?"

"Just now. This moment."

"Not 'when': 'how,'" said O'Rourke.

"I was looking for a skirt's handbag, she'd come back to fetch it."

"There was a bit of a scrap," said MacCormack. "You had other things to do."

"I'd just found it when things started getting rough."

"And?"

"Just at that moment, I had a sort of intuition."

Callinan jumped:

"An *ankou*[1]?"

They all became extremely interested.

"What're you talking about?" asked MacCormack.

O'Rourke shrugged his shoulders. Without a word, he went and replaced Callinan at the window. Outside, the British had quietened down and were thinking things over; they were

---

1. See note, p. 39. M.P.

giving no sign of life. Night was falling. Callinan went over to Caffrey.

"An *ankou*?" he asked him again.

"Yes," said Caffrey. "Bullets were whistling all around. They were coming in everywhere."

"What about Kelleher and Gallager?" asked MacCormack, anxious about the fate of his men.

"Doing fine," replied Caffrey.

He went on: "So, while the enemy was attacking us, I felt something inside me telling me that one of them was hiding hereabouts. So I made straight for the lavatory. It was locked. I heard someone breathing on the other side."

"What about our victims?" asked MacCormack.

"I don't think they've moved," replied Caffrey.

MacCormack turned to O'Rourke.

"Is the girl still out there?"

O'Rourke lowered his eyes.

"Yes. Someone ought to throw a blanket over her. She's indecent."

"We'll get rid of all three of them," said MacCormack.

"And then what?" Callinan asked MacCormack.

"Was it really an *ankou*?" MacCormack asked Caffrey.

Without looking round, O'Rourke said:

"If there's really someone down there, we'll have to do something about it."

"Yes," said Caffrey, answering MacCormack. "It was as if I heard a voice telling me that."

"I'll come down with you," said MacCormack to Caffrey. "You stay here, the rest of you."

He took out his revolver.

Callinan said to Caffrey:

"You must tell me more about it later."

MacCormack and Caffrey went out of the room and, very slowly, started to go downstairs. They passed Dillon, who was bringing up a case of ammunition.

21

HEARING footsteps on the stairs, Kelleher and Gallager looked round. They saw MacCormack and Caffrey going downstairs, very slowly, Colts in hand. They turned left, into the corridor. Night was falling. The streets were deserted. The British were still giving no sign of life. No light dared show itself. A bit of moon appeared above the roofs. The Liffey began to ripple gently. The town was very silent.

Then Kelleher and Gallager heard a woman's scream. They turned round. There were other more muffled sounds. Then another female scream, exclamations and oaths. Next, in the half-light, they saw a shadow being dragged in by their two comrades, a shadow that was barely struggling and had stopped screaming.

"What's going on?" asked Gallager, with some emotion.

"A skirt hiding here," said Caffrey. "We're going to inter-rogate her."

"Why don't you just chuck her out?" asked Gallager.

"Oh, by the way," said MacCormack, "someone ought to throw a blanket over the girl in the street."

"What about the other two," said Gallager, "why don't we chuck them out too? With a blanket over them."

"Then we're going to interrogate her?" asked Caffrey.

MacCormack and Caffrey had come to a halt, and Ger-trude was standing with her back to the wall. Each holding one of her wrists. Her head bowed, she didn't say a word.

"Put a blanket over the girl outside," said MacCormack. "The others can wait."

"It makes my hair stand on end," said Gallager, "to think, just like that, that I'm going to spend the night with a couple of stiffs."

"We could sling them out," suggested Kelleher. "Put them in a little pile at the corner of the street while the British are snoozing."

"You oughtn't to be afraid of the dead," said MacCormack. "Any more than of the living."

"Are we going to interrogate her?" demanded Caffrey. "Are we going to ask her questions?"

"I'll go and throw a blanket over the girl outside," said Gallager.

"Wait until it's quite dark," said MacCormack.

Gallager stuck his face against the loophole they'd fixed in the barricading of one of the windows.

"If I screw my eyes up," he said, "I can just see her mortal remains. She looks as if she's waiting for a lover. It's beginning to obsess me. It does obsess me. And there's the other stiffs in their little cupboard, they'll be coming out later, riding on broomsticks and floating awhile in the air while they do be groaning. They'll have green faces and false shrouds."

He turned round to MacCormack.

"I don't like it. We ought to chuck the lot in the Liffey. Including the girl."

"We aren't murderers," said MacCormack. "Come on, Gallager—courage! Finnegans wake!"

"Finnegans wake!" replied Gallager, dry-mouthed.

Stifled sobs were heard. Caffrey had just run his hand over Gertie's buttocks.

"I told you to be correct," MacCormack reproved him.

"She may be hiding a gun."

"That's enough."

Dragging Gertie with them, they started to climb the stairs. Gertie stumbled, but didn't resist. She had immediately stopped crying. The two look-out men on the ground floor watched them going up. Then they returned to their guard duty. Night had really fallen, now, and it was a very dark night, breached by the light of the full moon.

"A towser," Gallager suddenly murmured.

And he added:

"He's sniffing her. The lowlived cur."

He shouldered his gun and pulled the trigger.

That was the first shot of the night. It reverberated strangely in the silence of the insurgent town. The dog yelped. It made off in a lamentable state, howling more and more pathetically. A bit farther on there was a second shot, then calm reigned once again. A British bullet had put the cynical animal out of its misery.

"What a shit-house, all these corpses!" said Gallager.

Kelleher didn't answer.

22

A FEW SECONDS later, Gallager said:

"D'you think *we*'ll be able to question her, too?"

Kelleher didn't answer.

Gallager was afraid his courage was going to forsake him. He didn't press the point, and the conversation died a natural death. He took advantage of this to lend an ear.

23

THEY HAD lighted a little candle. Dillon was on guard duty at a window. MacCormack was sitting at Sir Théodore Durand's table; Larry O'Rourke was on his right. Callinan and Caffrey were standing on either side of Gertie, whom they had put on a chair and tied up a little, but taking precautions.

"Name, Christian name, occupation?" said MacCormack.

He turned to O'Rourke and asked: "Is that right?" Larry nodded. MacCormack also asked him: "Shall we write it down?" But the others said: "No point." So MacCormack repeated:

"Name, Christian name, occupation?"

"Gertrude Girdle," replied Gertrude Girdle.

She had sat in this same chair in front of that same table on other occasions, but then that armchair had been occupied by an esteemed civil servant of a certain age, who nourished with the chickweed of affection the doves of a discreetly platonized desire. But Sir Théodore Durand had been done in (she didn't know it), and here she was face to face with a Republican who was very certainly a terrorist.

Didn't make a bad impression, however. Though not very well dressed.

The other one, beside him, really all right. Undoubtedly a gentleman. Clean nails.

To her right, to her left, louts. Real Republicans, these. They'd tied up her wrists. Though it was true, without hurting her much. Why?

At the window, another rebel, holding a rifle. He didn't make such a bad impression either.

All five of them were rather handsome men. With the exception of the interrogator's assessor, however, they were certainly not well-bred.

And most likely none of them had ever sung *God Save the King*,[1] the boors.

"Occupation?" MacCormack demanded once again.

"Young lady postal clerk."

"A real young lady?" said Caffrey, who had his own opinion.

"Which department?" asked MacCormack.

"Registered letters."

She was looking at them without fear, now. *They* couldn't see her very well. It was obvious that she had masses of blond hair, and that it had been cut short, which was odd. She was tall, and the candlelight projected faint glimmers on to the two protuberances in her blouse. Her face began to relax. At first, it had been almost ugly. Now, her unpainted, but bitten, lips showed the two thick accolades of their sensuality. Hard blue eyes. Straight nose, no quivering. MacCormack, flummoxed by the registered letters, said meditatively:

"Ah yes, registered letters."

Caffrey privately thought they ought to ask the damsel about the workings of this department. She made him suspicious. Dillon and Callinan, severe but fair, were suspending their judgment of the situation.

MacCormack turned to Larry O'Rourke. The intellectual visage of his lieutenant seemed to be covering, with an epidermal veil, a thought in the throes of fermentation. So MacCormack appealed to Caffrey.

"She ought to explain why she was where she was," said Caffrey.

Gertie blushed. Surely they weren't forevermore going to

---

1. English popular song. After singing it, you take leave of one another. M.P.

remind her of the shame of this retreat, all the more so as the said retreat had been involuntary. Thinking of it once again, since they were forcing her to, she turned crimson.

"We might perhaps leave that detail on one side," said MacCormack, much embarrassed.

He blushed very red, even becoming cherry-red. O'Rourke still seemed to be thinking profoundly. But the three others started laughing, in a vulgar and rather impolite fashion.

Gertie began to cry.

MacCormack banged on the table and started to shout, thereby lightening his color.

"I never stop telling you," he yelled, "that we have to be correct. Melancholy God, I never stop telling you, and here you are making a joke of the fact that the young lady had a misfortune she's ashamed of!"

Gertie was sobbing.

"We may be rebels," MacCormack roared, "but we're still correct! And we are especially correct where ladies are concerned! Finnegans wake, comrades! Finnegans wake!"

MacCormack rose to his feet.

All the others stood to attention and declaimed, in chorus and with decision:

"Finnegans wake!"

"How dreadful!" murmured blonde Gertie, through her great big beautiful tears.

MacCormack sat down again, as did Larry. The others relaxed.

Dillon said to Callinan:

"It's your watch, now."

"Don't disturb the interrogation," said Caffrey.

"Yes," said MacCormack.

"Hang on a moment," said Callinan. "It isn't much fun having to hold her."

"You might be more polite to the young lady," said Larry O'Rourke.

"Don't understand," said Callinan.

"Shut your traps," said MacCormack.

"None of this," said Caffrey, "none of this explains any-thing. If there was nothing wrong with her, what the fuck was she doing in the bog, this tatty totty, who calls herself a young lady postal clerk? Eh? What was she playing at in the jakes, this useless numskull of a half-witted English nanny-goat?"

"That's enough," said MacCormack.

He thumped, rethumped, rerethumped, and rererethumped, his fist down on the tablecloth, and consequently (indirectly) on the table.

"That's enough! That's enough!" said he.

However, addressing himself to the damsel:

"Even so, it *is* fishy."

Gertie looked him straight in the eyes, as a consequence of which he felt a (slight) stirring in the region of the bladder. This surprised him, but he didn't mention it.

"I was powdering my nose," said Gertie.

MacCormack, whose gaze was still firmly glued to the gaze of this girl, didn't immediately grasp the meaning of her reply. But Caffrey, whose comprehension of his incomprehension was more rapid, asked sharply:

"Doing *what* to your nose?"

"Powdering it, you boor," replied Gertie, encouraged by MacCormack's look which, she thought, seemed to be throwing her a line.

MacCormack, who was indeed highly perturbed, did feel his look being translated into a (hard) line. Larry O'Rourke was experiencing a similar development but, being more intellectual than his chief, he only perceived tensions of lower-voltage in his physiology. But his heart was equally engaged. Neither had as yet realized the similarity of their convergences. "Powdering my nose," Gertie repeated, "yes, powdering it, you abject Irish terrorist! And anyway, let me go! Let me go! I tell you to let me go! Untie my hands! Untie my hands!"

Once again her sobs sobbed.

MacCormack scratched his head.

"We might perhaps, indeed, untie her hands," said he.

Said he. MacCormack. With circumspection.

"Perhaps," said Larry O'Rourke.

"Yerra," said Caffrey, "but she's capable of manhandling us."

"I should have come off watch a quarter of an hour ago," said Dillon. "Shit."

On hearing this word, Gertie's sobs retripled.

"Go on," said MacCormack to Callinan.

"Do we or do we not untie her?" asked Callinan.

"Nothing doing," said Caffrey.

"That's enough," said O'Rourke.

"Well then?"

They listened to her crying.

The serene night was clasping the dazzling moon in her sooty thighs, and the soft down of her constellations was lightly stirring in the breath of a classic breeze transmitted by the Gulf Stream. The civilians, terrorized by the terrorists, had gone to earth in their private territories, and the soldiery, leveling their weapons, were respecting, for strategico-tactical reasons, the calm of these nocturnal hours, which owed all their obscure clarity to the dispersed presence of some two thousand stars, not counting the planets and their satellites, the most relatively considerable of which is, beyond the shadow of a doubt, the one mentioned above.

When everything is as silent as this, it goes straight to the heart. Or, even lower down, to the copulatory organs. O ethereal music of the spheres! O erotic power of the cosmic semi-quavers, effaced by the fatal gravitational inclination of the world towards nothingness!

On the polished, transparent surface of the silence, Gertie's tears fell, one by one, crystalline and salty.

The rough rebels began to realize that correctness was

constituted of a certain reserve (meaning that there are certain-things-you-Kant-do), or, at the very least, of a certain mastery over one's primitive reflexes.

They sighed, while she sobbed.

"We'd got as far as the powder," said MacCormack.

"Do we or don't we untie her?" asked Callinan.

"And what about me coming off watch?" asked Dillon.

"Oh shit," said O'Rourke. "Let's be serious."

"Yes," said Caffrey. "Let's interrogate her."

"Miss Girdle," said MacCormack, "you were speaking of powder. We are waiting for your explanation."

"Powder!" exclaimed Caffrey. "Yes, powder! We'd like to know what that means!"

With her hands tied, Gertie couldn't wipe away her tears, nor stop those running down inside her nostrils.

She sniffed.

MacCormack felt the stirrings of tenderness in his heart.

"Lend her your handkerchief," he said to Caffrey.

"My what? You must be joking."

He always ejected his snot without any material aid.

"Here," said Callinan.

He pulled out of his pocket a big green handkerchief adorned, in its four corners, with golden harps.

"Fuck!" exclaimed Caffrey. "Talk about elegance!"

"A present from my fiancée," Callinan explained.

"Which one?" asked Caffrey. "The waitress at the Shelbourne, or the one at the Maple?"

"Pothead," said Callinan, "it was all over with the Maple one a month ago."

"Then it was Maud who gave you that?"

"Yes. She's a good nationalist."

"And in any case, she's well stacked. Lucky sod."

Larry O'Rourke took the floor:

"Have you finished?" he asked coldly.

MacCormack intervened:

"Well then, blow her nose," he said to Callinan.

Callinan looked embarrassed. He muttered:

"That'd muck up my present. My beautiful silk harps, they'll get all draggled with this English girl's snot. I don't want to. I refuse."

He carefully refolded his scarf and stuffed it back in his pocket. Faced with this act of indiscipline, MacCormack frowned.

Highly displeased.

So he turned to Larry.

"You do it."

"It's a job for a medical man," said Caffrey, aside.

O'Rourke gave him a severe look. Caffrey adopted a detached one. O'Rourke stood up, walked round the table and approached the girl. He took a handkerchief out of his pocket, a fairly clean handkerchief, but O'Rourke had had it for at least three days as he didn't use it much, not having a halituous skin and never—you might almost say—having a cold. He unfolded this toilet accessory and gave it a sharp shake to expel the scraps of tobacco or of various fibers that might have become lodged therein.

Gertie Girdle contemplated these preparations with horror.

24

SHATTERED by the shimmering reflections of the moon in the waters of the Liffey, Gallager started thinking out loud, and he said:

"I'm hungry."

"Yes," replied Kelleher, "I could do with a bite to eat."

Gallager jumped.

"What did you say?"

"I said I could do with a bite to eat. The provisions are in that room over there."

"And what about the corpses?"

"They can stay where they are."

"Would *you* go in there?"

"Aren't you hungry?"

Gallager moved away from the loophole and, in the half-light, went over to Kelleher. He sat down beside him.

"Oh, those corpses, those corpses . . ."

"Leave 'em be."

"And that girl out there. I can't stop looking at her. There haven't been any more dogs. I count up to two hundred, and when I get to two hundred I allow myself a glance at her. She still looks as if she's waiting for a man to come and get on top of her. Do you think she was a real young lady? And got herself croaked before she'd ever made love?"

"Shit," said Kelleher. "I'm hungry. Did you notice? I think there's some lobster."

"And the girl up there?" murmured Gallager. "Do you think they're interrogating her? You can't hear a thing."

"Maybe they're going to interrogate her tomorrow."

"No. They must be interrogating her now. Listen."

They listened.

"You can't hear a thing," sighed Gallager.

"They're doing it quietly," said Kelleher.

"What d'you mean?"

They were speaking in very low voices.

"We'll go up and interrogate her later," replied Kelleher.

He laughed very softly.

"What d'you mean?"

"Pothead. Here, I'm hungry. Shall I bring you some lobster?"

"What a job!" Gallager growled. "It wouldn't be so bad if it wasn't for the corpses."

"Want me to wake them up?" asked Kelleher.

Gallager shuddered. He got up and went back to his post. A glance showed him the dead girl. The moon continued on her course. The Liffey was sending its silvery fish-scales gliding down between the quays, allegedly deserted but in fact haunted by the enemy soldiers. Gallager took a deep breath, thought of his country's future, and said to Kelleher:

"That's right; some lobster."

25

THE OPERATION accomplished, O'Rourke carefully refolded his handkerchief and put it back in his pocket. He went and sat down beside MacCormack again. There was a silence.

Dillon went over to Callinan and said:

"All the same, you're not going to tell me it isn't your turn, now."

Callinan didn't answer. He went and took Dillon's place. He looked out through the loophole, saw the Liffey sending its silvery fish-scales gliding down between the quays, allegedly deserted but in fact haunted by the enemy soldiers, and he seemed to hear a decisive masculine voice pronouncing the word "gliomach" which, translated from the Irish, is lobster. Then he realized that he was hungry. But he didn't say anything.

MacCormack coughed.

"The interrogation will continue," he said.

Gertie seemed to have calmed down again. She had regained her British courage. She felt strong, and sure of herself. Besides, she was now convinced that they were not going to ask her any more questions about her sojourn in the lavatory, or insist on knowing the reasons why there-she-was and there-she-stayed.

She raised her eyelids, then, and rested her blue gaze on the physiognomy of Larry O'Rourke, which blushed, but Larry O'Rourke himself didn't flinch. He leant over to his chief and said something to him in a low voice. MacCormack nodded his approval. Larry, turning to the prisoner, said:

"Miss Girdle, what is your opinion of the virginity of the mother of God?"

Gertie examined them all with a circular glance, and replied coldly:

"I'm well aware that you're all papists."

"We're all whats?" asked Caffrey.

"Catholics," Callinan explained.

"Then she's insulting us!" said Caffrey.

"Silence!" yelled MacCormack.

"Miss Girdle," said O'Rourke, "will you please be good enough to answer my question with a yes or a no."

"I've forgotten what it was," said Gertie.

Caffrey saw red. He shook her by the arm.

"She's taking the piss!"

"Caffrey!" howled MacCormack. "I told you to be correct!"

"Even so, we aren't going to let her go on taking the piss out of us much longer, are we?"

"*I* am conducting the interrogation at the moment," said O'Rourke.

Caffrey shrugged his shoulders.

"Let me have her for an hour," he murmured, "and we'll see whether she still feels like making fun of us."

Gertie raised her head and examined him. Their eyes met. Caffrey blushed.

"Miss Girdle," said O'Rourke.

And Gertie turned her head in his direction.

"I asked you whether you believe in the virginity of the mother of God."

"In the?" asked Gertie.

"Virginity of the mother of God."

"I don't understand," said Gertie.

"It is in fact a mystery," remarked Dillon, who was fairly well up in the catechism.

"She doesn't know the mother of God!" exclaimed Callinan, with contempt.

"She certainly is a protestant," said Caffrey, with indifference.

"No," said Gertie, "I'm an agnostic."

"A what? A what?"

Caffrey had begun to panic.

"An agnostic," O'Rourke repeated.

"Well well," said Caffrey, "we're certainly learning some new words today. Anyone can see we're in the land of James Joyce."[1]

"And what does it mean?" asked Callinan.

"That she doesn't believe in anything," said O'Rourke.

"Not even in God?"

"Not even in God," said O'Rourke.

There was a silence, and they all considered her in terror and consternation.

"That isn't quite accurate," said Gertie, in a soft, sweet voice, "and I think you are simplifying my thought."

"The bitch," murmured Caffrey.

"I do not deny the possibility of the existence of a Supreme Being."

"Fuck," murmured Caffrey. "Now we're for it."

"Make her shut up," said Callinan.

"And," Gertie continued, "I have the greatest respect for our gracious King George the Fifth."

Once again, silence and consternation.

"But look here," MacCormack began.

He did not, however, continue. Sudden bursts of machine-gun fire came rattling against the wall, and the panes of the barricaded windows went splintering out into the street. On the ground floor, Kelleher's machine-gun started rat-a-tat-tatting back. A few bullets slid through the loopholes and started buzzing around in the room.

---

1. There is a slight anachronism here, but Caffrey, being illiterate, could not have known in 1916 that *Ulysses* had not yet appeared. S.M.

The men fell flat on their stomachs and crawled over to their weapons. Gertie's chair was knocked over backwards, and the girl started wriggling and writhing in her uncomfortable position. Thus, she revealed slender but substantial legs, tightly draped in that precious material, silk. Larry grabbed his gun, and then crawled back to her and pulled her skirt down over her ankles. Then he went into battle. At which point Gertie realized that there was already one of them who was in love with her.

26

"GOOD THING we'd finished the lobster!" said Gallager, as he spotted a shadow behind a pile of wood.

Kelleher fed in another belt.

Gallager fired. The shadow tottered.

"Stupid cunts, moving about like that at night," said Gallager. "It'll only make more corpses, whose souls'll come and torment us."

He fired again. The shadow, tottering badly, fell into the water on the other side of the bridge and went plop.

"That one," said Gallager, "will get his soul eaten by the lobsters."

Kelleher fired a few bursts, sending out a spasmodic spray of bullets. There was a respite.

"I wonder what's happening to the girl upstairs," said Gallager dreamily.

But once again, the shadows had begun to move.

27

SEVEN mares were entered for this race. After they'd been paraded they were tied together side by side. They were black, with superb, glistening cruppers. But they never stopped kicking and fighting each other. The one who was farthest to the left finally managed to strangle her neighbor with her front legs. The imprint of a gorilla's hand was discovered on her neck. Because the future criminal had been taken to the Zoological Gardens.

As we know, Dublin's Zoological Gardens are about three quarters of a mile from the entrance to Phoenix Park, and about half a mile from the North Circular Road tram. Nearby are the People's Garden, the Garda Síochána H.Q., and the Marlborough Barracks. It isn't a very large zoo but it is nevertheless worth a visit, for it is extremely well laid out. The star-turn, if we may so term it, is the lion house, which contains eight cages. As for gorillas, there were none at that period. But it was not this implausibility that awoke Commodore Sidney Cartwright, but an insistent knocking on his cabin door.

He stirred, and called come in. Which is what was done by a sailor who stood to attention and held out a message. Cartwright decoded it. And thus he learnt of the Dublin insurrection.

The *Furious* had orders to sail up the Liffey and, if necessary, to bombard the various points indicated, and in particular the post office on the corner of Eden Quay.

Cartwright got up, and began to behave like the good

British naval officer that he was. Which, however, did not stop him worrying about the fate of his fiancée, Gertie Girdle. The telegram, naturally, didn't speak of her. It was official, general and synoptic, and in consequence had no reason to bother its head with particular individuals.

A few moments later Cartwright was standing on his poop deck with a heavy heart, a lumpy throat, an empty stomach, a dry mouth and a glassy eye.

28

THE FIGHTING had stopped as it had started, for no apparent reason. The British didn't seem to have made the slightest progress. They had certainly lost several men. No one in the Eden Quay post office had been hit. On the first floor, after several minutes' silence, the five men exchanged glances. MacCormack finally decided to say that it seemed to be over, and Larry O'Rourke agreed with him.

"Shall we go on with the interrogation?" asked Caffrey.

The girl was still lying on the floor, tied to her chair, but keeping still.

Dillon went over to pick her up but O'Rourke got there first. Grasping Gertie under the arms, he set the whole lot back on its six feet. For a moment he allowed his hands to linger under her warm, slightly moist armpits. He removed them slowly and, as casually as you like, passed them under his nose. He paled a little. Caffrey, imperturbable, was observing him.

O'Rourke went and sat down beside MacCormack again. MacCormack had let himself fall into his chair: he was sleepy. He rubbed his eyes.

"Let's get on with it," he said. "Caffrey, isn't it your turn to go on watch?"

"Yes," said Caffrey. "I'm going. This interrogation gives me a pain in the arse. It isn't a bit like I thought it would be."

He went and took up his position at the loophole, and from then on his eye stayed glued to this interstice in their military architecture. MacCormack turned to Larry.

"Well, are you going on with your questions?"

"We already know she isn't a catholic," said Callinan.

"She doesn't believe in anything," added Dillon.

"Even so, we surely aren't going to waste all our time tormenting this girl," said Callinan. "We ought to be thinking about having a kip, chief. We're going to have a hard day tomorrow. Our insurrection isn't just a joke."

There was a strange silence. O'Rourke raised his head and said to Callinan:

"Well said, Callinan. You're right. You've got the right idea. I still have one or two more questions to put to the young lady, though."

"Sure, five minutes one way or the other aren't going to make any difference to us," said Callinan.

Caffrey, over in his corner, shrugged his shoulders. He pulled a feather out of a protective cushion and started to pick his teeth, still staring at O'Connell Bridge which, as it happened, was deserted.

"Well, go on then," said MacCormack.

O'Rourke collected his thoughts, and said:

"Miss Girdle, just now you made a profession of faith which was somewhat aggressive, or, to say the least, tinged with atheism. Nevertheless, you seem to have rejected any accusation of scepticism, if I have correctly understood the true meaning of the phrases you uttered, interrupted as you were by certain reflections made by my companions in arms."

Caffrey didn't budge. O'Rourke continued:

"Yes, you do not seem to reject all the attributes of the God in whom we believe. Wherein do your reservations reside, Miss Girdle? In Royalty?"

Without raising her eyes, Gertie inquired:

"Who are you, to interrogate me in this way?"

"We are combatants, we are the Irish Republican Army," replied O'Rourke, "and we are fighting for the freedom of our country."

"You're rebels," said Gertie.

"Certainly. That is very precisely what we are."

"Rebels against the English Crown," Gertie continued.

In his irritation, Caffrey dropped his rifle on the floor. Gertie jumped.

"You've no right to be rebels," she declared.

"She's overdoing it," said Callinan. "Let's lock her up in the next room and get some rest, ready for when things get really serious."

MacCormack yawned.

"One more minute," Larry insisted. "It is very interesting for us to get to know our adversaries."

"As if we haven't known them for centuries," retorted Dillon, who was beginning to doze off.

"She believes in the King but she doesn't believe in God!" exclaimed Larry. "Isn't that strange and fascinating?"

"It's certainly odd," said MacCormack in a detached manner. "But," he added casually, addressing Gertie, "do you really think your King is as good as all that?"

"He looks like a numskull," said Callinan.

"Show her his portrait," said MacCormack. "She can't see it."

Callinan climbed up on to a chair and unhooked the photograph of the King from its place on the wall facing the desk. A stray bullet had shattered its glass and nibbled away a corner of its frame. The object was beginning to lack dignity. Callinan propped it up against a filing cabinet and moved the candle, so as to give it adequate light.

Gertie looked at the portrait.

"No one could say he looks very bright," Larry O'Rourke commented. "Nothing in his face radiates either intelligence or energy. And that mediocre personage is the symbol of the oppression of hundreds of millions of human beings by a few tens of millions of Britons, but the oppressed no longer swoon in ecstasy at the sight of that insipid face, and you see here and now, Miss Girdle, the first consequences of this critical judgment."

"That's really talking," said Callinan approvingly.

"All I have to say is: God save our King!"

"But you don't believe in God. So who's going to save him?"

"What a dope!" exclaimed Callinan.

"She'll end up taking herself for a Joan of Arc," Dillon remarked.

"But," yelled MacCormack (he yelled, so as to shake off the drowsiness creeping over him on all sides), "but we keep telling you that your King is a stupid cunt! As witness the fact that he can't beat the Germans, that the Zeppelins are bombarding London, that millions of English soldiers are getting themselves killed in the Artois just to let the French establish their dominion in Europe. Which isn't very clever!"

"That's true," Gertie conceded.

"You see! And all Ireland knows that he indulges in the solitary vice, and that it makes him so moronic that he's incapable of understanding the slightest connection. Absolutely."

"Do you really think so?" asked Gertie.

"Absolutely. A poor sire, a poor wretch, that's what your King is. In short, I repeat: he's a stupid cunt!"

"But," cried Gertie, "if the King of England is a stupid cunt, then we can do whatever we like!"

29

"ARE WE allowed to get a bit of sleep?" Kelleher suddenly asked.

"I'm not sleepy," said Gallager.

"What's the time? The moon's going down."

"Three o'clock."

"Do you think they'll attack again tonight?"

"No idea."

"I wouldn't mind a bit of a kip."

"Have one, if you like. I'll keep watch."

"Is it allowed?"

"Get some rest, old chap, if you feel like it. I don't."

"You aren't sleepy?"

"No. Not with all these corpses."

"Forget them."

"That's easy to say."

"It's quiet, up there," Kelleher remarked.

"Do you think they're asleep?"

"Don't know. Did you see the girl's face, when they brought her out of the lavatory?"

"No. The only face I see is the one of the kid out there on the ground, in the street, in the dark."

"Forget it."

"That's easy to say."

Gallager suddenly jumped.

"No, Kelleher, after all, don't go to sleep, please don't. Don't leave me alone. Don't leave me alone with all these corpses."

"Right, I won't go to sleep."

"Mind you, I wouldn't mind lying down beside the girl out there; I didn't say on her, but it's the two Brits next door that torment me. They can't like us. And then, they must be upset, being dumped there like that. Sure, they're our enemies, but what good does it do to humiliate them?"

"You get up my nose."

Kelleher stood up.

"Here, I'm going to treat myself to a nip of uisce beatha."

"You can pass it on to me."

They took several gulps, and drained the bottle.

"And tomorrow," said Kelleher, "there'll be some more."

"Some more what?"

"Corpses."

"Yes. Maybe us."

"Maybe. I wouldn't mind a kip."

"I'm scared," said Gallager. "Those dead men are so close to me."

He sighed.

Kelleher picked up the uisce beatha bottle and chucked it against the wall. Where it discreetly broke.

"I've got an idea," said Kelleher.

Gallager belched interrogatively.

"Tell us, then," said he.

"Well," said Kelleher, "what we have to do with the corpses, we have to liquidate them."

"How so?" hiccuped Gallager.

"By chucking them into the liquid element. You saw that chap you picked off, he fell into the drink right away, and now he's not bothering you any more. So I've got a suggestion to make: we shove them all in the wheelbarrow, or one by one if there isn't room for them all, and we go and chuck them in the Liffey. Then tomorrow, when the British turn up, they'll find us nice and rested and free from care, just as free as our Ireland will be when we've won."

Even before Kelleher had got to the word "won," Gallager exclaimed: "Yes, yes. That's what we'll do," and he started gyring and gimbling in the most highly disorganized fashion. He added:

"That was my idea! That was my idea!"

"It'll be dangerous," Kelleher remarked.

"Yes," said Gallager, becoming immobilized in uffish thought. "With the others, we could just run over to the quay, but it's the girl, on the pavement there, to pick her up ..."

"Yes," said Kelleher, "that won't be any picnic."

"And what about MacCormack," said Gallager, "what's he going to say about it all?"

"We'll just paddle our own canoe. It'll be an act of initiative."

"Yerra. Ah well. And anyway, I can't go on living like this till I die."

"You help me put the two civil servants in the wheelbarrow, then you start pushing the girl. When you're just at the water's edge, I rush up and we toss the lot into the water at the same time, so there's only one plop. Then we run back, and that's it."

"It's nice of you to entrust the girl to me. I like fresh meat," said Gallager, meaning this as a joke. He was feeling slightly cheered up at the very proximate possibility of getting rid of three ghosts at one stroke.

"To work, then," cried Kelleher.

They abandoned both watch and machine-gun and, with fair precision, in spite of the darkness, went over to the little room where the two civil servants had been stored. Kelleher sacrificed himself and opened the door, which he did noiselessly; the two boyos were waiting peacefully. They started with Sir Théodore Durand, and put him in the wheelbarrow. Next they went and fetched the doorman. At this point they realized that it was going to be difficult to stick the two corpses in the same means of locomotion; having reflected for quite some time, they decided to put them head to foot.

Then they unbarricaded the entrance door. Kelleher half-opened it and Gallager crawled towards the street, flat on his stomach. He let himself glide down the steps and, after a few snake-like movements, found himself very precisely nose to nose with the dead girl. He couldn't see her very clearly. It seemed to him that her eyes were half-closed and her mouth half-open, he looked away, in the direction of the zenith. A lot of stars were shining, the moon was disappearing behind the roof of the Guinness Brewery. The British were nowhere to be seen. The Liffey was making little lapping sounds as it washed against the quays. Things, then, were thus: dark and calm.

Gallager, after this survey of the situation, looked once again at the little cadaver. He reconstructed her face, with his recent memories. He thought he recognized her. It was her all right. Having identified her, he stretched out his arms and started to push her. He was surprised to encounter a certain resistance. One hand was placed on a thigh, the other on an arm. Both were cold. Gallager persisted, and the corpse rotated. The thigh hand found itself on a buttock, the arm hand against a shoulder blade. Gallager dragged himself along a few more inches and pushed again. From one buttock his hand moved on to the other buttock, from one shoulder blade on to the other shoulder blade. And so on.

Gallager was having a hard time, he was scarcely paying attention to what his paws were palpating, he felt neither terror nor desire. It was her bootees that got on his nerves, every so often they made a noise, with their high heels.

He was sweating all over by the time he reached the edge of the quay. All he had to do now was give one more shove, and the corpse would be precipitated into the Liffey. He could sense the coolness of the water. The nearby lapping sound seemed crystalline, the tinkling little bells of this nocturnal river-line. What was uppermost in Gallager's mind was the British, who were becoming more than ever his mortal enemies, in that he felt himself distinguished amongst all the other insurgents. He had completely forgotten the agreed tactic, so his heart nearly failed him when he heard an appalling, bombastic noise.

When Kelleher had worked out his plan he had forgotten the steps outside the entrance door. Rushing out with his wheelbarrow he couldn't keep it balanced on the way down, its contents had toppled out and gone flop, and Kelleher had come a cropper, performing a magnificent somersault, accompanied by the sonorous clatter of the vehicle.

Gallager's sweat went back through his pores to where it had come from. Pale and wan, the darkness must have made him look grey. His muscles contracted and his fingers tetanically penetrated the flesh of the deceased young lady post office clerk. At this moment he was holding one of her shoulders on the right, one of her flanks on the left. He began to think of all kinds of things, and everything was gyrating beneath his closed eyelids. Shots began to ring out. Gallager pressed himself against his burden and clasped it frantically in his arms, babbling:

"Mother, mother . . ."

Bullets were whistling, but they were fairly few and far between. It was clear that they were being fired by men who were half-asleep, with slow reactions.

"Mother, mother . . ." Gallager went on stammering.

He didn't even hear the wheelbarrow coming over the cobble-stones. The heroic Kelleher had stuck the two civil servants back in his wheelbarrer and was making a dash for it, under the enemy fire.

The moment he was within low voice reach, he started yelling, sotto voce:

"Chuck her in then, you cunt!"

Gallager, overcome, ceased his spasmodic transports and,

with a single shove, precipitated the young lady into the drink, where she fell at the same time as the other two corpses and the wheelbarrow itself. There was a quadruple plunge, and Kelleher, immediately turning on his heel, galloped back to their blockhaus. Gallager, without thinking, stood up and did likewise.

A few more shots were fired, but they missed the two amateur morticians.

They cleared the steps in a couple of bounds and dashed through the gaping, somber entrance. Kelleher rushed over to his Maxim and let off a few random bursts. Gallager, as he shut the door, could see the wheelbarrow, still floating, drifting with the current down the Liffey.

30

RIGHT from the beginning of the engagement, Callinan had been wondering what he was supposed to do. He was dozing, a rifle between his legs, squatting outside the door of the little office in which they had decided to shut their prisoner, a solution which, in any case, had only been adopted after a somewhat muddled discussion. Callinan couldn't really see the necessity for him to stay outside this door; he considered that it was his duty to fight, not to be a jailer. He was extremely curious to know what was going on. He stood up and, after a few instants' hesitation, turned the handle and slowly pushed the door open. The room was faintly illuminated by the lights coming from the night outside. Callinan made out a desk, an armchair, a chair. A stray bullet sent the window pane flying in splinters. He flattened himself instinctively and then, cautiously raising his head, he discovered the English girl pressed up against the wall by the window, watching what was going on outside with intense interest.

The battle died down, and Callinan stood up. He asked in a low voice:

"You aren't wounded, are you?"

She didn't answer. She didn't even jump. And then they heard the quadruple plunge.

"What's going on?" asked Callinan, without budging.

Still watching what was happening outside with the same intense interest, she signed to him to come closer. At this moment the fusillade started up again with greater intensity. As Callinan cautiously sidled up to her along the wall he heard two men running, the ground floor door closing, and the bursts from Kelleher's machine-gun. He was now very close to Gertie. She felt for one of his hands, and squeezed it very hard. He looked out over her shoulder. He could see the quays, with their piles of wood, O'Connell Bridge and, finally, the Liffey, flowing slowly, carrying with it towards its mouth a vacillating wheelbarrow.

"What's going on?" he asked again, in a very low voice.

She went on squeezing his hand. With the other, he was still holding his rifle. The battle continued, shots were ringing out. Callinan decided to use his gun.

"Let go of me," he murmured in Gertie's ear.

This time, she turned to face him.

"What have they done to her?" she asked.

"To who?"

"To the other one."

They were whispering.

"Which other one?"

"The girl who was lying out there in the street."

"Oh! The one who got herself knocked off by the English? One of your lot."

"They threw her into the Liffey."

"Ah, so that was it."

"And one of them was lying on top of her, earlier, one of your lot."

"What was he doing, lying on top of her?"

"I don't know. He was sort of jerking up and down."

"And then?"

"I don't know. And another one, another one of your lot, was running, pushing a wheelbarrow."

"And then?"

"They threw lots of corpses into the Liffey."

"Could be. And then?"

"All that plunging. I saw it all. I heard it all. And you've slain Sir Théodore Durand, haven't you?"

"The postmaster?"

"Yes."

"I think so."

"They threw him into the Liffey, too, with another one, and with the girl, the one whose stomach your colleague was jerking up and down on."

"And then what?"

"Then what?"

She looked at him. Her eyes were extraordinarily blue. She added:

"I don't know any more."

And then she put her hand on his codpiece.[1]

"Look, over there, look at that dead men's wheelbarrow, drifting with the current down the Liffey, to go and catch cod in the Irish Sea."

He looked. And indeed, there was a wheelbarrow floating in the river. He uttered a little moan, to signify that he had seen it. The hand placed on his codpiece remained *in situ*, immobile and pressing, not such a small hand at that, fleshy, rather, and its warmth was beginning to penetrate the material of his clothing. Callinan didn't dare budge, but not all his body obeyed the injunction of his will, one part rebelled.

"Well yes," said he, "it's floating, the wheelbarrow is."

Gertie ran her hand over the shaft of the human handcart that was taking fright by her side.

"Why haven't you killed me?" she asked. "And thrown me into the water, after rolling me over the cobble-stones, like the other girl?"

"I don't know," Callinan stammered, "I don't know."

"You're going to kill me, aren't you? You're going to kill me? You're going to throw me in the river, like my colleague, and like Sir Théodore Durand, who loved me so respectfully?"

---

1. A part of the masculine costume, extremely common in Ireland. M.P.

A shiver ran down her spine, and she pressed nervously, but vigorously, what she held in her hand.

"You're hurting me," Callinan murmured.

He freed himself and took one, and then two, backward steps, but not three. Gertie's silhouette was outlined against the sky framed in the window. Gertie was now standing quite still, her head turned towards the Liffey. A light nocturnal breeze was ruffling her hair. There were stars all around.

"Don't stay at the window," said Callinan. "The British will shoot at you. You make a fine target there."

She turned to face him; her silhouette disappeared. And now they were both in the dark.

"Well," she said, "so you intend to turn this country into a republic, do you?"

"We explained that to you earlier on."

"Aren't you afraid?"

"I'm a soldier."

"Aren't you afraid of being beaten?"

He felt that she was looking very precisely in his direction. In any case, they were only two paces away from each other. Callinan began to retreat slowly and very silently. He spoke a little more loudly so that she shouldn't realize the difference in the distance.

"No," he replied, "no, no, and no again."

He increased the volume of his voice with every backward step he took. He found himself with his back against the side wall.

"You're going to be beaten," Gertie retorted. "You're going to be crushed. You're going to be ... you're going to be ..."

Callinan, having hoisted his rifle all the way up his body, now shouldered it. There was a little glint at the end of its barrel.

"What are you doing?" Gertie demanded.

He didn't answer. He was trying to imagine what was going

to happen, but he couldn't, and the little glint wobbled indecisively.

"You're going to kill me," said Gertie. "You decided to on your own initiative."

"Yes," Callinan murmured.

Slowly, he lowered his gun. MacCormack had been wrong to keep this crazy girl alive, but he, Callinan, had no right to kill her. He propped his rifle up in the corner. He had both hands free, now. Gertie advanced towards him, feeling the darkness with her outstretched arms. She was quite tall. She made contact at the level of his armpits. Callinan's jacket was unbuttoned, he wasn't wearing a waistcoat. Gertie started by kneading his ribs, and then gradually descended to his waist. At which point Callinan's arms closed round the English girl. She pressed herself against him and put her arms round him underneath his jacket, caressing his muscular shoulder blades. Then she ran her fingers down the bony, knotty path of his spine and, with her other hand, started unbuttoning his shirt. She could feel the moist flesh of the Irishman, whose pectoral muscles were quivering under her fingers. She rubbed her face against a shoulder that smelt of gunpowder, sweat and tobacco. Her hair was tickling the rebel's face. A few blond, flowing strands even floated up his nostrils. He wanted to sneeze. He sneezed.

"You're just as much of a stupid cunt as the King of England," Gertie murmured.

Callinan thought so too, for, while he did not hold the British monarch in high esteem, he nevertheless considered it prodigiously blameworthy and stupid to be holding in his arms a female of the English race, the cause of all the miseries of his nation, and a hellish spoilrebellion. If it weren't for her, everything in this little post office would be so simple. They'd simply shoot at the British, piff paff, and there, clearly laid out in front of them, would be the path to glory and Guinness, or, conversely, to a heroic death. Whereas what had happened was that this clot, this twat, this mischief-maker, this mort, this goose, this gaby, had gone and shut herself into the double-you-see at the vital, tragic moment, and here they were stuck with her on their hands, and you could say that again, on their rebel hands, an unbearable burden, and perhaps even a speculatrix.[2]

He was now quite clearly a prey to shudders, spasms and surgescences which reminded him that he was only a poor sinner, a man of flesh, but he was still thinking of his duty, and of the need for correctness enjoined by John MacCormack.

Meanwhile, Gertie had discovered the Irishman's navel. She had been incited, both by statues and by hearsay, to believe that this part of the human body was identical in men and women. She was not, however, quite sure, enamored as she was of her own umbilicus, into which she took pleasure in introducing her little finger, for the purpose of rubbing its depths, an occupation she found particularly delightful and feminine. Given that in men it was identically similar, she thought, only vaguely however, that it was doubtful whether it would be so deep and so soft.

She was charmed by that of Callinan, which she discovered was just as delightful to tickle as her own. As for Callinan, who was a bachelor, he knew little of the blandishments preliminary to the radical act, never having hunted anything other than fubsy totties, or slatterns harvested on piles of hay or tavern tables still greasy with everything. He found this caress hard to bear, therefore, and began to foresee that this series of gestures would lead to a quite different conclusion from that of an honest refusal. But where would this conclusion take place?—that was what he was asking himself, now that he found himself in extremis. He still had one

---

2. Latinism (from *speculatrix*, female spy). Untranslatable into French which, as everyone knows, is a somewhat inadequate language. M.P. (English must therefore be a somewhat less inadequate language, for this word can in fact be found in our dictionaries, even if only as an archaism. B.W.)

penultimate scruple: the social level of his Iphigenia, and then one ultimate one: the girl's virginity. But then, thinking that this maidenhoodity was perhaps no more than probable, he abandoned all thought and devoted himself without *arrière-pensée* to the sexual activity triggered by the provocation of the young lady post office employee.

31

"READY about! Hunt to starboard! Hoist the portholes! Slip the poop! Harvest the mizzen-royal!"

Having given his ultimate orders, Cartwright went below to the mess-room where he found Teddy Mountcatten and his first officer swigging whiskey with a melancholy air. Even though he strongly disapproved of the rebellion of the Republicans who claimed to be Celts, he would infinitely have preferred to be fighting the Germans on the high seas, rather than to be bombarding a few Dublinesque civilian buildings which, after all, were part of the British Empire.

"Hallo!" said Cartwright.

"Hallo!" said Mountcatten.

Cartwright helped himself to a big glass of whiskey. To which he added a minute quantity of soda water. For a few moments he gazed at the transparency of the glass, following with a vague eye the carbon dioxide bubbles which . . .

He had doubts about the chemical nature of these bubbles. He inquired of Mountcatten:

"Carbon dioxide?"

And, with his eyes, he indicated the lightweight spheres hoisting themselves up from the depths of the tumbler to the surface of the liquid.

"Yes," replied Mountcatten, who had been at Oxford before joining the Royal Navy.

After half an hour's silence, Mountcatten went on:

"This is no sort of job."

Three quarters of an hour later, Cartwright asked:

"What isn't?"

After having reflected for quite some time, Mountcatten completed his thought:

"They're swine, of course, these Irish Republicans. Even so, personally, I'd rather be bombarding the Huns."

Mountcatten had a certain tendency towards loquacity, but he was even more given to self-control; he said no more, but lit his pipe with a disciplined air—not manifesting the slightest emotion, that is to say.

Cartwright, having emptied his tumblerful of whiskey, began to think of his sweet fiancée Gertie Girdle, the young lady postal clerk at Eden Quay, Dublin.

32

CALLINAN, too, had begun to think of his fiancée. His eyes flickering, he thought for a moment that he could see, fluttering a few inches away from his eyelids, the pretty little mug of Maud, the waitress at the Shelbourne. If all went well, if, that is, an independent and national Republic was established in Dublin, he was going to marry her in the autumn. She was a real Irish girl, was little Maud, and decent, and nice.

But all these thoughts didn't stop Callinan committing an abominable crime. And in any case they arrived too late, these thoughts, this ideal of a faithful betrothal. Too late. Too late. The British virgin, spread-eagled on a table, legs hanging down and skirts tucked up, was sniveling over her lost maidenhood, which astonished Callinan for, after all, she'd certainly been asking for it, he reckoned. Maybe, though, she was sniveling because he'd hurt her; and yet he'd been careful to do it with the least possible brutality. His wicked deed accomplished, he remained motionless for a few seconds. His hands were still exploring the body of this girl and he thought it odd that she had so little on under her dress; certain details even surprised him strangely. For instance, she wasn't wearing any drawers, or any frilly, Irish lace petticoats. She was certainly the only well brought-up Dublin girl who thus disdained dishabilles with layers and complications. Maybe, Callinan told himself, it was a new fashion, imported from London or Paris.

This disturbed him immoderately. His loins were on fire. He gave three or four jerks and then, abruptly, it was all over.

He withdrew, in great embarrassment. He scratched the tip of his nose. He pulled out his big green handkerchief with the Irish harps embroidered in all four corners, and wiped himself. He thought it would be kind to render the same service to Gertie. Gertie had stopped sniveling, and was lying still. She shivered slightly when he dabbed at her, very delicately. He put the handkerchief back in his pocket and did up his buttons. Then he went and fetched his rifle, which he had put down in a corner, and tiptoed out of the room.

Gertie had stopped sniveling, and was lying still. Her thighs were shining milkily in the greyish rays of the dawning day.

33

"THERE are two lowlived dogs in our midst," said Mac-Cormack.

Callinan looked around him.

"Two lowlived dogs?" he asked. "Two?"

"You've got a funny sort of look," O'Rourke said to him.

"What about the girl?"

"I locked her in," Callinan replied.

He sat down, his rifle between his legs, automatically stretched out a hand, grabbed a bottle of uisce beatha and took a great swig, followed by another, barely less copious.

"Which are the two lowlived dogs?" he asked again.

He looked around him.

The day was dawning. What a short night it had been. And still this silence, this British calm. What was the matter with the English, then, why were they corrupting this rebellion with their shifty, silent hanky-panky?

Very high up in his lungs, in the region of his sirloin, Callinan felt an enormous anguish molesting his respiration.

He looked around him, noticed Gallager and Caffrey dozing beside a little castle of empty Guinness bottles and decorticated tins.

"Those two?" he murmured.

"No," replied MacCormack.

"Why aren't you still guarding the English girl's door?" O'Rourke demanded.

"I told you, I locked her in," replied Callinan, irritated.

RAYMOND QUENEAU

"And anyway," he went on, "which are the two lowlived dogs?"

"I thought you'd been given an order," said O'Rourke. "To guard the young lady."

Callinan felt like retorting that she wasn't quite so much of a young lady as she had been, but he abstained.

"It's probably all right if she's locked in," said MacCormack.

"And what if she starts signaling from the window?" O'Rourke objected.

Caffrey grunted.

"All we have to do is lock her in where she was to start with."

"All right," said Callinan, "I'll go back."

"One man less," said MacCormack. "We're going to need everyone we've got."

"Let's have her in here with us," said Gallager. "We'll all guard her."

"That's an idea," said MacCormack.

Callinan thought very fast (and it can't even be called thinking any more, when someone thinks as fast as that) and, without giving O'Rourke time to express his opinion, he rushed off to fetch Gertie. At the door, however, he stopped and asked:

"Which are the two lowlived dogs?"

But he didn't stay for an answer.

34

HE WASN'T sure that one of the two wasn't him. But if so, who was the other? Who was he, and what on earth could he have done, the other one? As for him, Callinan, no, of course not, the others couldn't know. Maybe one of them had been listening at the door? But in that case, MacCormack would have made much more of a fuss. Because what he, Callinan, had done, was the lack of correctness to end all lacks of correctness. Even so, it wasn't entirely his, Callinan's fault.

When he reached the door he took the key out of his pocket, but his hand started trembling and the key kept dancing up and down around the lock. His throat was dry, and he couldn't wait. He propped his rifle up against the wall, and, finally finding the keyhole with his left hand, he managed to get the passe-partout in, and turned it. He pushed the door which, slowly, opened. He forgot his rifle.

The sun had risen now, but it was still hidden behind the roofs. The early morning was grey and misty. Clouds were passing by. Over Trinity College way, the attics of the houses were gently turning red. Gertie, her legs tucked back, was lying on the table where Callinan had left her, and seemed to be asleep. She had pulled her skirt down a little, and nothing higher than mid-calf was visible. Her short hair was straggling half over her face and half over some blotting paper.

Callinan went up to her quietly, but without trying to be totally silent. The girl was lying still. She was breathing slowly and regularly. Callinan stopped, and leant over her face. Her eyes were wide open.

"Gertie," he murmured.

She looked at him. He didn't know how to interpret her look. She lay still. He stretched his two big hands out towards her and took her by the waist. Then, he slowly moved up towards her breasts. Just as he had imagined, she wasn't wearing a corset. This particularity, added to the fact that she also had short hair, once again disturbed Callinan no end. He could feel the straps of her brassière under her armpits: this sub-vestimentary detail completed his confusion. All these feminine novelties seemed to him at the same time marvelous and dubious. So it must be the latest fashion, but how could this simple young lady Dublin post office clerk keep up with it so well in the middle of a war? All this must originate in London, or even perhaps in Paris.

"What can you be thinking about?" Gertie suddenly murmured.

She smiled at him sweetly, a little mockingly. Callinan was disconcerted, he let go of her and was going to straighten up, but Gertie caught hold of him, grabbing his hips with her knees, and then, crossing her legs, she drew him towards her.

"Take me," she murmured.

And she added:

"For a long time."

35

"WELL THEN," said Kelleher, "so MacCormack was beefing, was he? As if this was the moment to think about such things."

Dillon was dreamily cleaning his nails, and Kelleher was caressing his Maxim. A ray of the rising sun set its barrel gleaming.

"It's still all quiet," Kelleher remarked. "I wonder whether battle will ever commence."

Dillon shrugged his shoulders:

"We're fucked."

He added:

"They're just letting us sweat, and when they feel like it they'll liquidate us."

He concluded:

"We're fucked."

Returning to another theme, he declared:

"MacCormack was exaggerating."

"What about?"

"About us."

"He suspects us of something."

"As if it was any of his business. He ought to do something about that damsel and leave us in peace. But there you are, he doesn't dare, he's trying to think about something else."

"Gallager couldn't wait."

Dillon shrugged his shoulders:

"The idiot. They won't do anything to the girl, they're all too chivalrous, except maybe your Gallager. But the others'll stop him. Obviously, it torments them, but they'd never do it. She'll still be pure when she gets out of their clutches."

"She'd be even purer with us."

Dillon shrugged his shoulders once again.

"I wish we could get on with the fighting," he sighed, "even though deep down I'm not all that keen on it. I really must love my Ireland, to let myself in for such an activity. Yes, let's get on with the fighting."

He stood up and clasped his companion in his arms. Kelleher stopped contemplating his machine-gun for a moment and smiled at him.

36

THE WIRELESS operator brought Commodore Cartwright a message. The *Furious* was to stop at Ringsend. The British attack was to start at seven o'clock. At ten o'clock, another message would inform the *Furious* of the strategic positions still occupied by the rebels, which she was then to bombard.

"If there are any left," remarked Mountcatten, to whom Cartwright communicated this order.

"It'll all be over soon. Then we shall be able to reserve our strength for the Hun U-boats."

"I hope so," said Mountcatten.

37

"WHAT THE fuck can he be doing?" grunted MacCormack. "Why isn't he back?"

"He's probably doing just that," Caffrey, now wide-awake, commented laconically.

"You mean he's fucking her?" said Gallager.

Slapping himself on the thigh, he let out his enormous laugh.

"Shut your traps!" said O'Rourke. "Dirty beasts."

"Oho!" said Caffrey. "Jealous?"

"Callinan wouldn't do that," said MacCormack. "And in any case, you can't hear anything. She'd be yelling, if he had evil intentions."

"Perhaps she likes it," said Caffrey. "Just imagine, maybe she asked for it!"

He had addressed this remark to Gallager. They both laughed.

O'Rourke stood up.

"Dirty beasts. Dirty beasts. Shut your filthy great traps."

"As if medical students didn't know a thing or two about filth! Prude! You prayed too hard to Saint Joseph last night!"

"That's enough!" MacCormack suddenly bellowed. "We aren't here to quarrel. Kindly remember that we are here to fight for the independence of our country, and probably to die."

"And in the meantime," Caffrey remarked, "Callinan is well and truly screwing the English girl. Listen."

They stopped talking, and heard a series of little mewing

sounds which very gradually turned into long moans, interspersed with irregularly spaced silences.

"It's true, though," Gallager murmured.

O'Rourke paled; it was a sort of greenish pallor. MacCormack intervened:

"Oh come on, it's a cat."

And O'Rourke, who wanted to keep his illusions, agreed:

"Of course it's a cat."

And Gallager, with an idiotic smile, repeated:

"Of course. A cat. A cat."

Caffrey guffawed:

"Maybe the totty's pulling its tail. Poor cat. I'll go and see."

He went out of the room. There was a series of strident, accelerating lamentations, then a vertiginous silence. This was the moment when Caffrey reached the door. Callinan's rifle was mounting guard all by itself. Caffrey went in. It was over. Callinan was trembling as he rebuttoned his trousers, and Gertie had jumped to her feet. Her face was radiant with satisfaction. She looked at Caffrey insolently. Caffrey thought she was beautiful.

And he didn't know what to say.

After a few seconds, his reinvestiture concluded, Callinan asked him, without the slightest affability:

"Well?"

Caffrey replied:

"Well?"

Gertie looked at them both with a lively eye.

Callinan said again, with the same presence of mind:

"Well?"

And all Caffrey could find to answer was:

"Well?"

Callinan, with less assurance, said:

"You didn't see anything, did you?"

"But we heard."

"I'm dishonored," murmured Callinan, overwhelmed.

"They think it was a cat. You can say it was a cat."

"Will you say that, too?"

Caffrey examined Gertie with great attention. She was still panting a little.

"Naturally it was a cat."

Callinan pulled his beautiful green handkerchief with the golden harps out of his pocket, and wiped his face.

"Goodness," said Caffrey, "your nose has been bleeding."

38

"HERE THEY come," said Gallager.

O'Rourke didn't look round. Gertie had just come in, flanked by Callinan and Caffrey.

"It *was* a cat," said Caffrey.

"Holy Jesus!" Gallager confirmed. "Here they come! Here they come!"

MacCormack darted over to one of the loopholes.

"Miss Girdle," said O'Rourke, who had recovered his serenity, "it must have been explained to you that we considered your presence here to be suspect."

"They're rushing over the bridge!" Gallager exclaimed.

"The swine," MacCormack confirmed. "And there are plenty of them."

"We have decided that you are to remain constantly under our collective surveillance," O'Rourke continued.

"Shall we fire at them?" Gallager asked.

Various machine-guns that the British must have cached in the piles of wood began to perorate. Shrill bursts of fire spattered the facade. On the ground floor, Kelleher began to retaliate. Caffrey and Callinan darted over to the windows and, with MacCormack and Gallager, started firing at random.

"Take cover behind the desk," O'Rourke ordered, "and don't move."

Gertie obeyed.

O'Rourke went and locked the door and put the key in his pocket. Then he joined the combatants.

The British seemed determined to liquidate the affair once

and for all. They were swarming on all sides. It looked as if they now held O'Connell Street. The Eden Quay rebels saw a file of prisoners, their hands in the air, that the others were marching towards Metal Bridge.

"Things are going badly," said Caffrey.

"It's our comrades from the GPO," MacCormack remarked. "I recognize Teddy Lanark and Sean Dromgour."

"Telephone," O'Rourke suggested.

MacCormack, abandoning his post, went over to the desk that had belonged to Sir Théodore Durand, deceased. He caught sight of Gertie, crouching behind it, her eyes closed. Taking every precaution not to tread on her he sat down, turned the appropriate handle and picked up the receiver. Having listened, he said, between two bursts of fire from the other side, and there was beginning to be a smell of gunpowder:

"There's no answer."

His companions went on shooting down the British. Perhaps they didn't even hear this incidental remark of their chief.

Nor did they notice the way he jumped, immediately afterwards. For their part, they were taking careful aim, and hitting their targets. The British were beginning to get in a wax. It was still impossible for them to deploy themselves on the bridge, or along the quays, without suffering losses amounting to more than 45 percent of their strength (which, militarily speaking, could still be considered brilliant, but only just). They still persisted, however, with the courage of their strength.

"Who's that?" said a voice at the other end of the line.

MacCormack lowered his eyes. His mouth was dry.

"By Jove!" the voice continued. "Answer me!"

A little electric current began running up and down his spine, circulating along his spinal cord with increasing frequency.

MacCormack, stammering slightly, declared:

"MacCormack here."

"Another bloody fucking swine of a rebel, I bet," retorted the voice. MacCormack didn't know which way to turn. Gertie's surprising (to him) activity, in conjunction with this insult, had not only left him speechless, but had also cut the ground from under his feet.

"Look here," he said, "look here."

"So you haven't surrendered yet, you haven't been ejected yet, you Papist Hun, you squirt."

MacCormack began to sigh.

"No, but what's got hold of you?"

"Fi . . . fifi . . . fifinnegans wake," MacCormack mumbled.

"What? What? What's all that crap?"

But MacCormack was now in no state to answer him. To stifle his moans, he sank his teeth into the mouthpiece.

"You're making a funny sort of noise," remarked the voice on the other end of the line.

It added, however, with solicitude:

"You're not wounded, are you?"

MacCormack didn't answer. The ebonite crackled.

"Good heavens!" yelled the voice. "What's happening to you?"

MacCormack dropped the receiver on to the table and let out a long wheezing sound. He distinctly heard the far-off voice, screeching and nasal-twanging, articulating:

"We're waiting for you to surrender, to surrender immediately."

And the same voice, off:

"Huh, he isn't answering. Perhaps he's dead."

With half-closed eyes he could see O'Rourke, Gallager, Caffrey and Callinan, industriously firing at random. They weren't taking the slightest notice of him. The smell of gunpowder was getting stronger.

He lowered his eyes and saw Gertie who, her work concluded, was once more burrowing down behind the desk. She was wiping her mouth with the back of her hand.

He hung up and, his knees trembling, stood up. He said:

"It was our comrades from the GPO we saw going by just now."

"We shall never surrender," declared O'Rourke.

"Of course not," MacCormack agreed.

Zigzagging slightly, he went and got his gun and, with his first shot, brought down a Briton who had had the temerity to wish to cross O'Connell Bridge.

39

"WE'RE FUCKED," Dillon murmured.

Kelleher didn't answer. He was gently caressing his machine-gun, which was slowly cooling off after the last alert.

Once again the British had retired in order to prepare the final liquidation. All that could be heard now was distant and sporadic bursts of fire.

"What effect does it make on you?" asked Dillon.

Kelleher replied:

"None."

He patted his machine-gun.

"A good little creature."

He added:

"If it isn't for this time, it'll be for another time."

"Oh!" exclaimed Dillon. "I'm not worried about our Motherland. Our Eire is eternal. Just like the Christian era. It's us I'm thinking about."

"Yes, it'll soon be all over, between us."

"And what effect does that make on you?"

"Had to happen sooner or later."

Dillon reflected:

"Maybe we'll get out of it . . ."

"No," said Kelleher.

"No? You really believe: no?"

"Yes, I really believe: no."

"Why?"

"We shall be killed, down to the last man."

"That's what you think?"

"We shan't surrender."

Dillon cracked his fingers:

"You're very brave, Corny."

Kelleher stood up and walked a few paces, meditatively.

"I wonder what happened upstairs."

"Upstairs? They've been fighting, just like we have."

"I meant: about the girl."

"I don't give a damn."

Then he raised his head:

"Is *that* what's worrying you?"

Kelleher didn't answer.

"The little bitch. She's a pain in the arse for us, here. She's going to make trouble for us. It's always the same, with women. I don't have to tell *you* how well I know them. *You're* too young. I've had twenty years to get to know them, in my trade. Hm. After you, it'll be my trade I'll regret most. Clothes, I used to like all that. Dresses, when they changed. Fashions, I mean, and materials, too, silk, lace, Irish raised point . . ."

He stood up, took Kelleher by the shoulder and clasped him in his arms.

"I shall regret *you*, you know."

He added:

"Are you really thinking about that bint upstairs?"

Kelleher gently, but decisively, disengaged himself from Dillon's embrace. And in silence. Then they heard Gallager's cordial voice:

"Well, my pretty pansies, are we having a lover's quarrel?"

"Me, I don't understand such goings-on," added Callinan.

"No one asked for your opinion," retorted Dillon.

"Pah!" said Gallager. "At the point we've got to. Have to be understanding."

"We came to fetch a case of ammunition and several cases of uisce beatha. Are there any left?" asked Callinan.

"Yes," replied Kelleher.

"And how's your morale?" asked Callinan. "Doing fine?"

"We're fucked, aren't we?"

It was Dillon who said that.

"We shall be killed down to the last man," declared Gallager, with a joyous levity that made the couturier feel sick.

"Something wrong, Mat?" Callinan asked him. "You surely aren't going to back down now, are you?"

"Out of the question. Out of the question."

Gallager and Callinan looked at each other, shrugging their shoulders. They went over to the storeroom.

"That was a marvelous idea we had," said Gallager, "when we bunged the stiffs in the drink. It took a great weight off my mind—it's quite at rest, now."

"Here's something new!" exclaimed Kelleher, who hadn't taken his eye away from one of the loopholes.

The others immediately shut their traps and became plunged in a great crystal ball of silence.

"They're coming!" Kelleher went on. "With a white flag. There's an officer marching behind them . . ."

"Are the British going to surrender, then?" asked Gallager.

40

MOUNTCATTEN found Cartwright studying his telegrams. "Everything is going marvelously," said the Commodore. "I have a feeling that the insurrection has been crushed. All the positions occupied by the rebels have been recaptured. All, or almost all. I'm just checking them. I have a feeling that it *is* all... The Four Courts, Amiens Street Station, the GPO, Westland Row Station, the Gresham Hotel, the College of Surgeons, the Guinness Brewery, Harcourt Street Station, the Shelbourne Hotel, all those have been recaptured. What's left? The Sailor's Home?—recaptured, according to telegram no. 303-B-71. Townsend Street Baths? (What an idea.) Recaptured, according to telegram 727-G-43. Et cetera. Et cetera. General Maxwell has done a good job, and liquidated the situation with energy, rapidity and decision, and with just that touch of leisureliness that characterizes our army."

"Then we won't have to bombard the Irish? I'd rather not. That would be a waste of some excellent shells that are only dreaming of going and pummeling the Huns."

"I am aware of your views on that subject."

The wireless operator came in, bringing yet another telegram.

"Just a moment. I must finish checking my list."

He finished it.

"The only remaining position is the Eden Quay post office," said Cartwright.

He took the telegram and read it. "And this is an order to moor fore and aft in front of O'Connell Street."

"Then we'll have to waste some shells, after all," said Mountcatten.

Commodore Cartwright suddenly looked a little somber.

41

MACCORMACK and O'Rourke went back into the post office. Callinan, Gallager, Dillon and Kelleher were waiting for them. They rebarricaded the door.

"Well?" asked Dillon.

"Naturally, they're demanding our surrender. They say we're the last ones. The insurrection has been crushed."

"Lies," said Gallager.

"No, I think it's true."

"I thought we were never going to surrender," said Kelleher.

"Who's talking of surrendering?" said MacCormack.

"Not me," said Kelleher.

"And what are their conditions?" asked Dillon.

"There aren't any."

"Well then? Will they shoot us?"

"If they feel like it."

"Who do they take us for?" said Gallager.

They considered this question for some moments, which produced a silence.

"And what about the English girl?" Kelleher suddenly said. "Why don't we at least get rid of her?"

"In any case," Larry O'Rourke remarked, "if we're going to get killed here, we can't involve her in such an adventure."

"And sure why wouldn't we?" asked Kelleher.

"She's a pain in the arse," said Gallager. "Let's give her back to them."

"That is more or less my opinion," said MacCormack.

"You're the chief," said Mat Dillon. "Let's chuck her out, then, and they can have her."

"There might be one objection," said O'Rourke.

"What objection?"

"No; nothing."

The others looked at him.

"What d'you mean?"

"Well, we don't want her to be able to say anything about us."

"What information can she give them? She can't even know how many we are."

"That wasn't what I meant, Mat."

"What *did* you mean?"

He blushed.

"She was a pure young girl. There mustn't be anything different about her . . ."

"What *are* you talking about?" asked Gallager. "Don't understand."

"It's quite clear, though," Dillon put in. "If you've all been jumping her, that would be bad for our cause. That'd provoke the British, and they'd eliminate all our comrades who've fallen into their hands."

"*I*'ve been perfectly correct," said Gallager.

"Me too," said Corny Kelleher.

"Me too," said Chris Callinan.

"Then let's shove her out and die like heroes," said Dillon decisively. "I'll go and fetch her."

He dashed out, and raced up the stairs.

"You haven't said anything, MacCormack," Kelleher observed.

"Let her go," replied MacCormack, with a vague, absent-minded air.

"What about Caffrey!" Callinan suddenly exclaimed. "He's alone with her upstairs."

O'Rourke paled visibly.

"Ah yes . . . Caffrey . . . Caffrey . . ."

The medical student was practically stammering. His hands were trembling.

than MacCormack. That beastly pansy Kelleher was persecuting them. And anyway, what was going on? And what had gone on? Once again Larry scrutinized Callinan's features: they weren't talking. Next, he came back to Kelleher, and perceived that Kelleher had suddenly lost all interest in the subject. Then MacCormack looked at his watch, and said:

"We've only got two more minutes to give them our answer."

"To get rid of the English girl," said Gallager.

Dillon appeared at the top of the stairs:

"She isn't there. She must have vamoosed."

Kelleher slapped him on the back:

"She's fubsy, isn't she! the girl upstairs."

Putting into practice the rational method of breathing that had been taught him by the great poet Yeats, O'Rourke was trying to reduce his emotions to zero. He also recited three *Ave Maria*s, as an auxiliary aid.

"That girl's having a strange adventure," Kelleher went on. "Just suppose we hadn't been decent fellows, good, clean-living heroes, can you imagine what the girl wouldn't have seen? Seen—that's just a manner of speaking."

With two supplementary *Ave Maria*s and one *Hail Joseph*, O'Rourke managed to answer:

"Some people have no right to talk about women."

"*I* don't butcher their corpses," said Kelleher.

"Let's not talk about such horrors," cried Gallager.

"Shut your traps," said MacCormack.

Once again they plunged into silence.

"The British must be getting restive," said Callinan, in a subdued voice.

No one answered him.

"John MacCormack," said Kelleher, a little later (no word having been uttered in the meantime), "John MacCormack, you don't seem quite at your ease. I know you haven't got the jitters, so what's the matter?"

Larry O'Rourke regarded MacCormack:

"It's true, you do look funny."

He was relieved that Kelleher was letting *him* off the hoo

"Yes," said MacCormack. "And so what?"

O'Rourke regarded him in anguish. He knew perfe well, and just as well as Kelleher, that MacCormack h got the jitters. Then what could be contorting his face ir an extraordinary fashion? The same thing that was ric' his own mug: the girl upstairs. His eyes left John an/ ined Callinan. But Chris's gaze was pure and blue. L: guish returned: he himself certainly had an even fui

42

THE BRITISH plenipotentiaries withdrew, and disappeared behind the piles of Norwegian wood. The rebels rebarricaded themselves in. It must have been around noon.

"Maybe we could have a bite to eat," said Gallager.

Dillon and Callinan went and fetched a case of tinned food and some biscuits. They sat down and started chewing in silence, like people who are in the process of becoming heroes and who no longer concede anything to the banality of existence except its extreme banalities, such as eating and drinking, urinating and defecating, but not the ambiguous games of language. If MacCormack had begun to speak, he would have said: "Why are you all looking at me like that, you can't know, you can't understand what happened." If O'Rourke: "Oh Virgin Mary, what can have become of her, it's idiotic, but I was falling in love with her." If Gallager: "Corned beef doesn't taste so good an hour before you die as it does a week before. But you have to nourish yourself when you're going to die." If Kelleher: "She's certainly the first woman that's ever interested me. Vamoosed—just as well. It'll be easier to be real heroes." If Callinan: "They're good comrades. They're pretending not to know what happened to me." But it was Dillon who spoke, and he said:

"They'll crush us like rats."

"Like heroes," Kelleher retorted. "We're aggravating the British a hell of a lot, even if we *are* supposed to be rats."

"Good comrades make good heroes," said Callinan.

"And so does good corned beef," added Gallager, slapping himself on the thigh.

"I wonder where she can have got out," murmured O'Rourke.

"It's a mystery," MacCormack concluded gravely.

A bottle of uisce beatha went the rounds.

"What about Caffrey?" Gallager asked. "Are we going to leave him in the lurch?"

"Take him something to eat and drink," MacCormack ordered solemnly.

"Or rather, tell him to come down," O'Rourke put in. "While we're waiting to Face the Last Fight, he might perhaps explain how he let the English girl get away."

"What the fuck can he be doing up there," said Callinan absent-mindedly.

For the sixth time, Dillon repeated his story:

"He was keeping a look-out at the window on the right of the office, he didn't look round. He said: 'The English girl? No idea.' I looked in the other rooms. I couldn't see anyone."

"Is that all?" Kelleher added.

"Maybe she went back to the lavatory," Gallager suggested.

"Why ever didn't we think of that!" MacCormack exclaimed.

They all stood up as one man (with the exception of Callinan, who was on watch), and then froze.

"Not all of you," said MacCormack to Gallager.

"Right, chief."

But a few steps farther, he stopped:

"I'm scared. What do I do?"

"You try and open the door quietly," MacCormack advised him. "You don't knock; that wouldn't be correct."

"We broke down the door, don't forget," said O'Rourke. "We smashed the bolt."

"And then?" asked Gallager, still undecided.

"*I*'ll go," Dillon declared. "No woman frightens me, in the lavatory or anywhere else. You can go and take Caffrey his lunch. He must be bored, all by himself up there."

"We'll come up in a minute," said MacCormack.

"I'll wait till he comes down," Gallager decided.

As he had begun to do a lot of thinking, he made another discovery:

"Maybe she beat it through the gardens of the Academy?"

"What a joke," O'Rourke replied. "Impossible."

"And what about the British," asked Kelleher, "couldn't they have got her out that way?"

"Impossible," O'Rourke repeated.

"Why's that?" Kelleher asked again.

"Because they're too slow-witted. It'll take them a week to discover that."

"And in a week, it'll all be over."

The uisce beatha bottle went the rounds once again.

Dillon reappeared. He said:

"I'm certainly out of luck. She isn't in the bog."

At this point Gallager decided to take Caffrey up his lunch: uisce beatha, dry biscuits and corned beef.

43

As the *Furious* passed the Southern and Western Railways goods station, Mountcatten said to his first officer:

"Nice town, Dublin: docks, a gasworks, goods trains, the polluted water of a little river."

"Which we won't have to demolish."

"I don't suppose the Eden Quay post office is an architectural masterpiece."

"It's odd that that should be the precise place where Cartwright's fiancée is employed."

"It seems to distress him."

"No doubt that edifice has some sentimental value for him."

"He isn't being asked to bombard his beloved."

"No, but he *would*: for the King."

Having invoked this personage, they stood to attention for a few moments. They were now passing the North Wall station, and troops on the platform, as well as civilians, waiting for their trains, watched them go by.

44

GALLAGER pushed the door open with his foot. Caffrey turned his head and said:

"Shove the stuff on the table and fuck off."

"Right, Cissy," Gallager stammered.

He shoved the stuff on the table, but even so he couldn't help watching Caffrey, who had already forgotten about him, so occupied was he with his present occupation. The latter concerned a girl spread-eagled under him on the table, legs dangling and hair disheveled, her skirt pulled up beyond her waist. Gallager's eyes abandoned their examination of the face and activity of his compatriot and transferred themselves to the feminine object lying underneath him, and very precisely to its long, white thighs, on which fulgurated the outline of a garter. It could only be a question of the young lady post office clerk, who was thus, abruptly and horizontally, making her reappearance.

"Well," yelled Caffrey, "haven't you vamoosed yet?"

He seemed far from pleased. Gallager jumped. He stammered: "Sure, sure, I'm going," and withdrew, backing out stealthily, his eyes still glued to the sleek, milky skin of the young British girl. What with the one who'd got herself knocked off the day before, and whose corpse must now be floating somewhere near Sandymount, Gallager suddenly thought that they certainly did have attractive thighs, all these girls in the Eden Quay post office. And that garter, whose slender, elastic outline seemed merely to have been made to render that flesh softer and more luminous.

Before he shut the door, Gallager tried to absorb all that beauty in one last look, and closed his eyelids in order not to let the image flee. He asked timidly:

"Couldn't I bring her up something to eat, too?"

Caffrey swore.

Gallager shut the door.

On the screen of his inner cinematograph he could still see the pure, phosphorescent and sensual forms of the English girl, and her vestimentary supplements: the taut stockings, the garters, the dress pulled up high. Once again, he conjured up the one who had perished on the pavement, and he began to mumble prayers in order to overcome temptation. He didn't wish to succumb once again to his penchant for purely personal satisfactions. He had come here to make Ireland free, not to give a jerk to the equilibrium of his spinal cord. After reciting some twenty *Ave Maria*s and at least as many *Hail Joseph*s, his loins felt softer. He was then able to go downstairs.

Even so, Dillon remarked: "You've got a funny look on your mug."

"Stop yelling!" the look-out man suddenly started yelling in a low voice.

Callinan was jumping up and down in excitement.

"This is it! Here they come! Here they come! The Royal Navy!"

45

THE *FURIOUS* moored fore and aft a few yards downstream from O'Connell Bridge. On Commodore Cartwright's order the guns were prepared to gun. But he still felt a certain reluctance to use them, not that he had anything against crushing Papist and Republican rebels, but this post office, whose functionary and almost Doric architecture was definitely ugly, greasy and sordid, this post office conjured up in his mind the engaging personality of his fiancée, Miss Gertie Girdle, whom he was to (and wished to) marry in the very near future, in order to consummate with her the act that was just a little intimidating to a chaste young man, the strange act whose occult peripeteia transforms a young bint from the virginal state into the pregnant state.

So Cartwright was hesitating. His sailors were awaiting his orders. Suddenly, half a dozen of them went sprawling on the deck, and a couple of others toppled over the rail and took a bloody header into the Liffey. They hadn't been on their guard. Kelleher had got fed up with seeing their self-satisfied silhouettes. His machine-gun functioned very well.

46

THE FIRST shell planted itself in the lawn of the Academy garden. Then it exploded, splattering grass and humus all over the statues copied from antiquity, plaster statues adorned with gigantic zinc fig leaves.

The second followed the same path. A few leaves fell.

The third landed in Abbey Street Lower on a group of British soldiers, which it destroyed.

The fourth carried off Caffrey's head.

47

THE BODY continued its rhythmic movement for a few more seconds, just like the male of the praying mantis whose upper part has been half-devoured by the female but who perseveres in his copulation.

At the first shot, Gertie shut her eyes. Opening them, possibly for no other reason than a certain curiosity about what was happening outside herself, a curiosity no doubt consecutive to a momentary appeasement of her desires, she perceived, her head being tilted to one side, that of Caffrey lying, severed, near a wicker chair. Then more things happened she didn't at first understand. But the kind of disembrained mannikin still surmounting her finally lost its momentum, stopped jerking and collapsed. Great spurts of blood came gushing out of it. Whereupon Gertie, screaming, wrenched herself free, and what remained of Caffrey fell inelegantly on to the floor, like a sawdust doll mutilated by the tyranny of a child. Gertie, now on her feet, considered the situation with some horror. She thought very rapidly: "That's one less." Fairly impressed, even so, by the dead, shell-devastated Caffrey, she retreated to the window, her thoughts in some disarray, trembling, covered all over with blood, and moist with a posthumous tribute.

She was really shaken. On the ground floor, the rebels were still obstinately shooting at random. A fifth shell exploded in the Academy garden. Gertie, averting her eyes from the waxy spectacle offered by the fragmented corpse, saw a British warship emitting fumes, though rather more from its funnels than from its guns. She recognized the *Furious*, and smiled vaguely: no one was there to ask her to explain her smile. A sixth shell, crashing through the roof of the house next door, demolished it. Rubble and bits of brick flew in all directions. Gertie became slightly alarmed. She moved away from the window, stepped over the corpse, went out of the room and found herself on the landing. Downstairs, in the half-light, the rebels, glued to their loopholes, were giving the sailors on the *Furious* quite a clobbering.

48

HE WASN'T absolutely certain that it was she; it was even unlikely. There could well be some fanatical republican amazon amongst them, but in that case, was it in good taste to kill a woman by means of bombs? Commodore Cartwright twirled his moustaches meditatively, and all the more so since Mountcatten had just told him that six sailors had already been killed and twenty-five wounded; as for the positive results of the demolition, they were slight. So Cartwright gave the order to cease fire, and sent a radiotelegram to General Maxwell informing him of the presence of a woman amongst the Eden Quay rebels, and asking for further instructions.

49

"ENTR'ACTE," Kelleher announced.

"They've quietened down," said MacCormack.

"I can't think what's got into them," said Mat Dillon.

"It gives us a bit of a breather," said Callinan. "We can comfort ourselves a bit."

Kelleher immediately started fussing with his machine-gun.

"What about Caffrey?" O'Rourke asked.

"I have a feeling there was a bit of a barney on the first floor," said Mat Dillon.

"Virgin Mary, Virgin Mary," murmured Gallager, holding his head in his hands.

"What's the matter with you?"

Gallager, trembling like a gun dog, began to emit little moans. Kelleher, abandoning his Maxim, patted him on the back.

"Come on, boyo," he said solicitously. "You aren't going to break down, are you?"

"Tell us about Caffrey," said MacCormack.

"I told you before," Dillon declared, "there's been some damage done upstairs. I'll go and see."

He went to see. As he set foot on the first step, he raised his head and saw Gertie, watching them and listening to them. She was holding herself very straight, with staring eyes, her crumpled dress covered in blood. Mat Dillon was very frightened. In a husky voice, he observed: "She hadn't gone," and the others looked round and saw her. Gallager stopped crying.

She began to move, and came down the stairs.
Dillon slowly turned back to face the group of his comrades.
She went over to them. She sat down.
She said to them, with great sweetness:
"I'd quite like a bit of lobster."

50

SHE ATE, and they watched her in silence. When she'd finished the tin she handed it to Gallager, who started fiddling
with it absent-mindedly. O'Rourke then offered her a tumbler
of uisce beatha, which she drank.

"Were you hiding?" demanded MacCormack.

"Is this an interrogation?" retorted Gertie.

She handed the tumbler back to O'Rourke.

"He's dead," she said. "His head's there," (she pointed) "and
his body's there," (she indicated a spot a little farther off). "It's
horrible," she added politely. "And the shell took part of the
wall with it, too. I'd like another glass of whiskey."

O'Rourke handed her another tumblerful, which she drank.

"Were you hiding?" MacCormack asked again.

"But Caffrey knew it," said Dillon, worried. "Was he lying
to me? Where were you, then?"

"Poor Caffrey!" said Gallager, beginning to moan again.
"Poor Caffrey!"

"Ask him," Gertie replied.

She pointed to Gallager.

"Did you see her when you took Caffrey his rations?"

"It's frightful, Virgin Mary! It's frightful."

MacCormack looked at Gertie with sudden and violent
anxiety.

"What have you done to him? It's all nonsense, about the
shell. Have you killed him? Have you killed him?"

"Go and look."

She was very calm, very calm. The others were keeping their distance from her. Callinan, the look-out man, kept turning round and staring at her in amazement. She smiled at him. After which he didn't move any more, and kept his eye glued to the loophole.

"Why are you smiling?" asked MacCormack.

But she had stopped smiling.

"I'll go and look," said Mat Dillon.

He was always glad of a chance to move about a bit.

"You'll be walking in blood," she told him. "It's horrible," she added politely.

"Virgin Mary! Virgin Mary!" Gallager kept mumbling.

Swearing at him, MacCormack and O'Rourke shook him. He calmed down. Turning his back on Gertie, he fetched his gun and went and took cover at one of the barricaded windows: nothing seemed to be happening aboard the *Furious*.

"What's the name of the ship that's bombarding us?"

They all noticed the *us*, but neither of the two look-out men answered. It was O'Rourke who informed her that it was the *Furious*, and he added:

"Why that question?"

"Ships don't all have the same name."

He didn't think she was being very nice to him.

"If," MacCormack went on, "if, how shall I put it, if you really had nothing to do with Caffrey's death, and if Caffrey really is dead, we shall surrender to the British."

Whereupon Callinan and Gallager jumped, turned round and looked at O'Rourke, who didn't understand why.

Gertie pretended to be considering the matter, and then answered:

"I don't want you to."

"Then you *were* hiding?" MacCormack asked yet again, obstinately sticking to his idea.

"Yes."

She immediately added:

"Caffrey knew it."

Gallager and Callinan took their eyes off her and again focused them on the *Furious*, where it was still all quiet.

MacCormack felt more and more ill at ease. He grunted:

"Caffrey, ah, Caffrey, ah yes!" and then fell silent, examining Gertie with anguish, madly afraid that she might suddenly and publicly decide to repeat her incongruous, not to say incredible, acts, whose confession is not even provided for in the catechism. But MacCormack had to admit to himself that he really didn't know what a priest could make a woman confess to; his gaze met Gertie's and he couldn't interpret it; so he shivered. He started grunting again, in totally unintelligent fashion: "Ah yes, Caffrey ... Caffrey ... ," then he suddenly decided: "I must come to a decision," he decided, and he started to exert his authority. Before anyone had had time to comment on his decision to come to a decision, he stood up, took Gertie by one arm and led the astonished girl over to one of the little offices (the very same one in which Gallager and Kelleher had deposited the corpse of the doorman), pushed her into it, and double-locked the door, thus demonstrating the firm-handedness of a leader of men.

He went back to the others and pronounced these words:

"Comrades and dear friends, this cannot continue. I'm not talking about the British, that's obvious, they're going to get us, we're fucked, mustn't kid ourselves, but even so, we're still going to give them a pain in the arse, we're still going to be heroes, sacred bloody heroes, we're still going to be the heroes to end all heroes, no doubt about that, but what's messing everything up is that girl, what an idea to go and hide in the lavatory just when battle commenced, no way of getting shot of her now, what she wants we don't know, but it's quite clear and plain to me that she has her own idea, what am I saying: 'her own idea'? Maybe even her own ideas, several of them. No. No. No. With this totty in our midst, everything's fucked up, we've got to come to a decision, a very clear, very plain decision, bloody melancholy God, and then it's not only that, but we've got to have it out amongst us, about her, we've got to tell the truth about her. That's what *I* think: I'm the chief, and I've come to a decision: first to come to a decision, which is my duty as your chief, and then, or rather in the very first place, that we should tell each other the truth about everything concerning that person of the feminine sex that I've just locked up in that little office."

This blether was followed by the silence to end all silences. It was such a silence that it even embarrassed the look-out men.

Callinan turned round and said:

"There's still no sign of life on the *Furious*."

A tenth of a second behind him, Gallager looked round and said:

"There's still no sign of life on the *Furious*."

Which caused a certain amount of interference, as when, in a physics lesson, one compares light with sound.

But none of the men present gave a roasted fart for interferences. They were giving their consideration to the crap John MacCormack had just been spouting. And the look-out men who, in the recesses of their guts, had retained the deeper meaning of his discourse, abandoned their hole-watching activities, at the disagreeable risk of being taken by surprise by a sneaky, surreptitious British attack.

Kelleher, scratching his Maxim's stomach, shattered the silence with these words:

"Seeing that you're the chief, go on then, and start, tell us the truth about everything concerning the human being you've just locked up and who isn't of the same sex as us."

"Very well," said John MacCormack.

He slid his right hand through the embrasure of his shirt and scratched the hairy skin of his belly.

Then he stopped, looking as if he was hoist with his own petard.

"By the way," said Kelleher, "what's Dillon up to? He's taking his time coming down."

51

CATCHING sight of Caffrey's head, some distance away from his body, and the whole weltering in blood, Mat Dillon, the Marlborough Street couturier, had fainted.

52

MACCORMACK coughed, stopped scratching his stomach, and said:

"Friends, Irishmen, countrymen—one thing is sure: that girl shouldn't be here. We'd have given her back to the British, just now, and that's what we ought to have done. But she hid. For what purpose? We don't know. She didn't wish to vouchsafe any explanation on that subject, therefore we can only make various conjectures. In short . . ."

"Yes, 'in short,'" said Kelleher, "so far you've just been talking boloney."

"In short," continued MacCormack, with bovine obstinacy, "as Larry stressed a few pages earlier, if we give her back, she mustn't be able to say anything to our detriment. On the contrary, it is necessary to our cause that she should acknowledge our heroism and the purity of our morals . . ."

Kelleher shrugged his shoulders.

"Therefore, she mustn't be able to say things. Therefore, nothing must have happened. And earlier on, you all said you had behaved correctly towards her. All except Caffrey, who wasn't there, and Larry, who asked the question, and . . ."

"And you," said Kelleher.

"Yes: and me. Well, *I* didn't say it, because if I had said it, I should have been telling a lie. *I* didn't behave correctly towards her."

Flabbergasted, Larry looked at MacCormack as if he were an extraordinary, unbelievable monstrosity. He thought he'd gone off his rocker. He hadn't left him for one single moment. How could it have happened?

"Or rather, the truth of the matter is that she didn't behave correctly towards me."

Now quite certain that MacCormack was mad, Larry immediately began to worry about practical matters: for the last bravura acts their little group still had to commit, they needed a real chief, not a mythomaniac, who was possibly even dangerous. It was up to him, now, to fulfill this role. But how would this transfer of power take place? This worried him. The three others were listening extremely attentively.

"The trouble is," MacCormack continued, "that there's nothing to prove it. It's a thing I can't give any details about. It's a thing I'd never come across. It's done. But as I say, it hasn't left any traces. So in that case, we can give her back to the British. She won't open her mouth on the subject I'm talking about."

"You're going a bit fast," said Gallager, "and I haven't got it. But your fancy confession isn't any good. If she wants to, that girl will open her mouth. And sure, the proof must exist. One of us raped her."

"How dreadful!" exclaimed Larry, forgetting his recent ambitions.

"Which one of us?" asked Callinan, in a pale voice.

"Caffrey," declared Gallager, in a dark voice. "Saint Patrick rest his soul!"

"That illiterate!" cried medic O'Rourke, in a cadmium-yellow voice.

"Well, shit then!" concluded John MacCormack, in an ocher voice.

"Caffrey," repeated Callinan. "Caffrey? Caffrey? Caffrey? Caffrey? Caffrey? Caffrey? Caffrey? How d'you mean, Caffrey? How d'you mean, Caffrey? But it was *me* that raped her."

He fell on his knees and went on whirling his arms around wildly. So wildly that it made him sweat.

"It was *me* that raped her! It was *me* that raped her!"

No one said a word, not even Gallager.

"*I* raped her! *I* raped her!"

The movement of his arms became slower and Callinan came to a kneelstill, looking totally overwhelmed.

"*I* raped her!" he repeated once more, in a less animated tone of voice.

"Or rather," he added, wiping his face with his beautiful green handkerchief with the golden harps, "or rather, *she* had *me*."

He leant his head in his folded arms on MacCormack's knees and began to keen.

"Comrades," he moaned, "my friends, she had me. She took my good faith by surprise; I'm a victim. Maud, my little Maud, my dear fiancée, forgive me. My heart is still faithful to you, the English girl only had my hide. My soul is still innocent, only my body is sullied."

"But this is absolutely crazy," Gallager yelled, "since it was Caffrey I saw."

He patted Callinan on the back in comradely fashion.

"You're getting ideas into your head, old man, you're dreaming, you never screwed the post office girl. You're not in your right mind. I swear to God it was Caffrey who raped her. And how he was raping her, at that!"

"Be quiet," murmured Larry O'Rourke, his face contorted. "Seeing that," he continued, "that he's dead now, and he's ascending into Purgatory, to disburden his lust in the arms of Saint Patrick, and we—we remain pure."

Callinan had stopped crying and had been listening carefully to the little oration of the native of Inniskea. He calmly asked him to specify the precise moment when he had seen Caffrey fornicating, and Gallager replied that it was when he had taken him up his *lón* (or lunch). MacCormack observed that in any case it could only have been at that moment. Whereupon Callinan uttered a triumphant cry:

"Well, me, I was the cat!"

He added:

"And the cat, that was a long time before, seeing that it was at dawn."

He stood up abruptly, and once again started flailing about vehemently.

"Eh? Don't you remember the cat? It was Caffrey who told me you thought it was a cat. And who advised me to tell you it was a cat. Well, the cat miaowing was Gertie, because I was giving her some sensations. And her virginity, I was the one who had it, that I'm sure of. Here's the proof."

And he brandished his big green handkerchief with its golden harps and its bloodstains.

Larry O'Rourke averted his eyes, so as not to have to see him any longer. He was indulging in some extremely difficult mental gymnastics in his efforts to appear calm, and not give any sign of the abominable feelings that were tormenting him. He felt he was in hell. He would have liked to cry like a child, but his role as deputy chief of a group of insurgents at the twilight of a failed rebellion forbade him to indulge in the tears of childhood. He had tried prayer, but it hadn't done any good. So he recited his osteology lecture notes, to give him something else to think about. But Callinan continued, with mounting exaltation:

"Not only was I her first, but I also gave her her second communion. And the second time, Caffrey caught me in the act. But we'd just finished. Luckily. It was him who advised me to say it was a cat."

"No no," MacCormack intervened, "the cat was just now."

Disconcerted, Callinan stopped short.

"And in any case," MacCormack continued, "the cat wasn't at dawn. It was a little later. At the precise moment when the British attacked. Your tale seems a bit muddled, to me."

"I'm telling you it was Caffrey," said Gallager. "I'm telling you I saw him."

Callinan dabbed at his forehead with his beautiful green, gold and red handkerchief, and sat down on an (empty) case of uisce beatha, shattered.

"But I'm quite certain I had her twice. Once at first, and another time next. The cat was the second time. The sensations, too. The first time, she didn't say a lot. She was very courageous. Must say, though, that she asked for it. Then, at the very most, she sniveled a bit. I wasn't brutal, but I do realize what a girl can suffer, at that moment. Don't you?"

Kelleher, who was keeping watch, answered, without looking round, that that was a question to put to Larry O'Rourke. Seeing that he had some medical knowledge, he ought to have some well-founded opinions on the subject. The student didn't reply.

He grabbed a bottle of uisce beatha, broke its neck brutally against the corner of a table, and poured a vast quantity down his gullet. This wasn't at all his normal practice, but he was on edge.

"And then, I usually do it with sluts who've had some terrific bulls and that you're more likely to get lost in. Me, that was the first time with a young person who hadn't had any experience of dalliance. What about you, have *you* ever known a girl in an intact condition like that?"

"You give us a pain in the arse," said Gallager. "I tell you, I saw Caffrey on top of her."

"Maybe. Maybe. But after. After my passage. And anyway, I've got proof. As much proof as you like. The proof to end all proofs. So much proof you won't know what to do with it. In the first place, this (and he brandished his snotrag like a flag). And then, the cat. And then, for example: I know what she wears underneath. I can tell you all about it. So that's one sort of proof. Yes, boyos, I can tell you what she wears under her dress. She doesn't wear drawers trimmed with Irish raised point lace, she doesn't wear corsets with whalebone busk, a real coat of armor, like ladies do, or all the squaws you may have undressed."

And MacCormack started musing about his wife (he hadn't so far had time to think about her), whom he had never undressed, and whom he had never seen undressing, and who was the great flabby mass he found in his bed at night. And Larry O'Rourke started musing about the women in Simson Street, with their negligées, their black stockings and their dirty pink garters, who otherwise weren't wearing a stitch, or very few stitches, so that it was gloomy even on a Saturday night. And Gallager started musing about the girls on his island who're dressed in rags and who get themselves impregnated in the shade of a dolmen or menhir without even so much as letting you get a glance at their nature. And Kelleher started musing about his mother, who always went about laced with cruel force into vice-like corsets, with the laces sticking out of her petticoats, which was what had led him to consider masculine codpieces much more aesthetic.

"No, with her, when you touch her here" (and he took hold of his own torso with both hands), "under her dress, it's skin you're touching, it isn't frills and flounces and whalebone busk, it's skin."

"Is all that true?" asked Dillon.

They hadn't heard him come downstairs. They'd been so engrossed.

"You certainly took your time," said MacCormack. "What were you doing?"

"I fainted."

After a stupefied third of a second, Gallager exploded. He was laughing like hell. He was crying with laughter.

"Don't forget there's a dead man in the house," Kelleher told him, without looking round.

Gallager cheesed it.

"Well?" MacCormack asked Dillon.

"His head had rolled quite a way away from his body. That did something to me. When I came to, I buttoned up his trews, I crossed his arms over his chest, I put his head in his hands, I covered him with a carpet and I said a few prayers for the repose of his soul."

"Did you remember Saint Patrick?" asked Gallager.

"And then I came downstairs. I wouldn't mind a drink."

Larry handed him the bottle of uisce beatha, and asked timidly:

"Why did you mention his trews?"

Mat was drinking; he shrugged his shoulders.

"So you see, I was right," said Gallager.

"And so was I," added Callinan.

Having liquidated the liquid, Mat sighed with pleasure, belched and sent the flagon flying with such abandon that it ended up fracturing itself against the letter box marked "Abroad"; and then Mat sat down.

They all began to meditate in silence. Each lit a cigarette, with the exception of MacCormack, who preferred to think by means of a pipe.

"There's not the slightest doubt," he finally articulated, "that we can't hand her back to them."

"Yes but even so, we can't kill her," said Gallager.

"What must she think of us," murmured MacCormack.

"Huh, for that matter," exclaimed Callinan, "we can think a few things about her, too."

"She won't talk," said Kelleher, without looking round.

"Why not?" asked MacCormack.

"Those aren't the sort of things a young lady can talk about. She'll keep quiet, or she may even say we're heroes, and what more do we want? As for handing her back to them, that's not what I'd advise. Let's simply forget about her, and let's just croak nicely, like men. Finnegans wake!"

"Finnegans wake!" replied the others.

"Well well," Kelleher continued, "it looks as though they're coming to life again on the *Furious*."

Gallager and MacCormack rushed over to their combat positions, followed by Callinan. Dillon stopped the latter as he went by.

"Is it true, what you were saying just now?"

"About the girl? 'Course it is. It's even a great pity that the British are trying to give me the chop, I'd have had some terrific memories, later."

"What you were saying. The way she was dressed."

"Aha! so you're interested?"

"I'll give them a bit of a going-over," declared Kelleher, and his machine-gun spat fire.

"Yes, I *am* interested."

Dillon let Callinan go and glue himself to a loophole, and went over to the little prison office.

MacCormack had left the key in the door.

The first gunshot rang out.

53

THE SHELL landed in the garden of the Academy. No doubt about it, their range still seemed to have a tendency to be too long.

Commodore Cartwright felt a pang of anguish.

54

THE SHELLS were beginning to come crashing down all around the Eden Quay post office, but still not on it, when Dillon went into the little office, having silently turned the key in the lock plate and pushed the door on its hinges, no less silently.

Gertie Girdle had spread her bloodstained dress out on a chair, for it to dry, no doubt. Sitting dreamily in an armchair she was dressed only in a brassière, in a girdle of the most modern type fabricated at that time, and in tight silk stockings, their seams strictly vertical.

On another chair, a slip was evaporating in a smoky atmosphere and, in so far as was possible, in Caffreyan purple.

Gertie's blue eyes were dreaming. She looked cold. And in fact her skin was granular, and the slight down, which in calmer times lay flat along her skin, was standing on end.

Dillon planted himself down in front of her and contemplated her, while Cartwright's men and Kelleher's comrades were attempting to compose a warrior symphony. Gertie raised her eyes and saw him, Mat Dillon. She didn't flinch. She said:

"And what about my wedding dress?"

"So it *was* you," Mat replied pensively.

"I recognized you."

"Me too."

"I didn't want to compromise you with your comrades."

"There was no reason."

"Meaning?"

"Thank you."

"But you're still thinking about it."

"I have every right to."

"Is it finished?"

"Quite finished."

"Have you seen this one?"

"Ruined."

"I'm cold."

"Clad yourself, then."

"What in?"

"In a trifle."

"In a carpet?"

"That isn't what I meant."

"Look here, I'm cold."

"I don't know."

"Do your job."

"Let me look at you."

"Please do."

"Callinan was right."

"Who's Callinan?"

"The one who . . ."

"Who what?"

"The one that . . ."

"That what?"

"Excuse me, I'm a gentleman."

"Is it true, Mr. Dillon, that you don't like women?"

"It is true, Miss Gertie."

"Aren't you sorry for me? When I'm so cold?"

"Let me look at you."

"You see. I don't wear a corset."

"I find that passionately interesting . . . You are the first . . ."

"Woman."

" . . . Young lady . . ."

"No: woman."

" . . . that I've seen adopting this new fashion."

"That could be."

"That *is*."

"And what do you think of it?"

"I'm not sure."

"Why not?"

"Old habits."

"That's idiotic."

"I know."

"Do you or don't you keep up with the fashion?"

"I do."

"Well then?"

"I told you . . . I find it rather disconcerting."

"Then my girdle doesn't send you into ecstasies? A girdle that comes from France, from Paris. And in the middle of a war, at that, I managed to get it. Aren't you in ecstasies?"

"Yes. All things considered, it's not bad."

"And my brassière?"

"Very elegant. And in any case, you seem to have attractive breasts."

"Then you aren't altogether indifferent to feminine charms?"

"I was speaking of them from the purely aesthetic point of view."

This was the only word of Greek origin that the Marlborough Street couturier knew.

"Well then," said Gertie, "I'll show them to you. I believe they really are very attractive."

She leant forward a little and passed her arms behind her back, with the graceful gesture of a woman unbuttoning her brassière. The object fell on to her knees, still swollen, and then flattened itself out. Her breasts appeared, round and firm, low set, their points erect, not yet purple from men's bites, but light-colored.

Even though both his profession and his mode of life had accustomed him to look with a cold eye at women in various stages of undress, Mat Dillon had to recognize the fact that he now occupied a slightly greater place in space than he had a few instants before. And he saw that Gertie had also recognized it. She stopped smiling and her gaze became hard. She stood up.

Flinging both arms out in front of him, Dillon took three steps backwards and stammered:

"I'll go and fetch you a dress ... I'll go and fetch you a dress ..."

And, turning on his heel, he ejected himself from the room and, his forehead cold and wet with sweat, found himself on the other side of the door, which he locked.

He remained there motionless for a few moments, to regain his calm. Then he set off. He shivered as he passed the LADIES' lavatory, whence had emerged this damsel, like Aphrodite from the waves. He came to a little door, which he unbarricaded. He found himself in a little courtyard. He propped a ladder up against the wall. A shell exploded not far away. Earth, gravel and rubble came showering down. He dropped over on to the other side. The Academy garden was strewn with craters. The statues copied from antiquity had all lost their zinc fig leaves and Dillon, as he ran, nevertheless cast a fleeting glance at the masculine endowments thus revealed. He thus felt he was back in a normal, healthy world, and, what was more, he observed that it was only the Venuses and Dianas that had copped it and were mutilated, and this made him smile. Another shell burst, less than a hundred yards away from him. The blast knocked him over. He got up. He wasn't wounded. He started running again.

The big bay windows of the Exhibition Hall had been broken. Dillon crossed the deserted Museum, without lingering to look at the daubs, which had been somewhat shaken by the bombardment. The gate giving on to Abbey Street Lower was open: the attendants must have fled when the insurrection broke out, not being overkeen on getting themselves done in for the sake of some mediocre treasures.

An abandoned tram. No one in the street. Hugging the walls, Dillon hurried off towards Marlborough Street.

55

"THERE'S something fishy somewhere," said MacCormack, stopping firing and putting his rifle down.

The others followed suit, and Kelleher stopped messing about with his machine-gun belts.

"It isn't natural," John went on. "It's almost as if they were doing it on purpose. They're blasting them off on all sides, but not on us. Anyone might think it was by mistake that they let off the one that carried off Caffrey's head—Saint Patrick rest his soul."

He went and got a bottle of uisce beatha, helped himself and passed it on. It came back to him empty. He lit his pipe.

"Callinan, go and keep watch."

The others lit a cigarette.

"If we're going to spend another night here," said Gallager, "I'd rather we buried Caffrey."

"To hell with the bloody brutal Sassenachs," Callinan suddenly said.

He hadn't looked round as he made his profession of faith; obeying orders, he was still keeping an eye on the environs, which latter gave no indication of any enemy presence. Every forty seconds the *Furious* was embellished with a little tuft of cotton wool at the end of its people-killing pipes.

"I wouldn't mind a shave," said O'Rourke.

They looked at each other. Their faces were grey, and covered with ugly stubble. And some of their gazes occasionally seemed to waver.

"Are you thinking of paying your respects to Gertrude?" asked Gallager.

"It's true, she's called Gertrude," O'Rourke murmured. "I'd forgotten that."

He gave Gallager an odd look.

"What makes *you* suddenly remember that?"

"Shut your traps," said Kelleher.

"Don't let's talk about her," MacCormack grunted. "We'd decided we wouldn't talk about her any more."

"What about Dillon? He isn't here," Kelleher suddenly observed.

They were amazed.

"Maybe he's up on the first floor," MacCormack suggested.

"Or with the girl," said Gallager.

"Him?" Callinan guffawed.

They could see his back trembling. Then he became quite still:

"I've had enough. To hell with the bloody brutal Sassenachs."

"It *is* odd, in fact," said O'Rourke. "It's almost as if they were sparing us."

He rubbed his hand over his cheeks.

"I wouldn't mind a shave," he said.

"Snob," said Gallager. "Do you want to impress Gertie?"

MacCormack brandished his Colt:

"Melancholy God! The next one who talks about her, I'll kill him. Got it?"

"Even so, we ought to bury Caffrey before nightfall," said Gallager.

"Where on earth can Dillon have got to?" said Kelleher.

"Maybe I can find a razor somewhere," said O'Rourke.

While the rest of them remained silent, he started walking up and down, searching in all the drawers, wherein he made nothing but mediocre discoveries.

"Shit," he said, "there's nothing."

"You don't really imagine," said Gallager, "do you, that the young lady post office clerks use Gillettes? You have to be an intellectual to get such ideas into your head."

"And what *I* say," said Callinan, "is: To hell with the bloody brutal Sassenachs."

"Why shouldn't they?" Kelleher retorted. "Dillon told me that some women—though it's true they're ladies, not post office clerks—shave their legs with Gillettes."

"You see," said Larry O'Rourke to Callinan, who still had his back to him, dutifully fulfilling his guard duty. He, O'Rourke, was still ferreting about, right, left and center.

"Me," said Gallager, "I reckon we even ought to bury him before twilight. Caffrey, that is."

"It even seems," Kelleher continued, "it even seems that some dames stick a sort of wax on their shanks, and when the wax has got cold they remove it, and their whiskers with it. It's radical, it's a bit painful, and then, really, it's only superladies who can treat themselves to such goings-on. Princesses, and that!"

"It's ingenious," said O'Rourke.

He was absent-mindedly fingering a stick of red sealing-wax.

"Try it then," Kelleher said to him.

"All things considered," said Callinan, "what I say is: To hell with the bloody brutal Sassenachs."

"We can't spend the night like that, with a corpse," said Gallager.

"I wonder where on earth Mat Dillon can have got to," said MacCormack.

"What with?" asked Larry.

"With what you've got in your hand."

"What a wag," said Gallager.

"Dillon may be dead," said MacCormack. "We hadn't thought of that."

"I'll melt it, and spread it over your face," said Kelleher.

"After that, you'll see how lovely and smooth your skin will be."

"We might well knock back another flagon of uisce beatha," said MacCormack.

A shell burst in the adjoining building. Bits of the ceiling disintegrated.

"To hell," said Callinan, "with the bloody brutal Sassenachs."

56

THE BOMBARDMENT had ceased. Larry was uttering abject moans of pain while Kelleher, sitting on his stomach to stop him squirming, removed the wax and the whiskers attached thereto, using a penholder for the purpose. Gallager and Mac-Cormack were enjoying this spectacle, while getting outside the contents of a tin of tuna fish. Callinan was still keeping watch on the *Furious*.

"Women don't make such a fuss," said Kelleher. "According to Dillon, at any rate."

"All things considered," Gallager remarked, chewing his oily fish, "their skin's tougher than ours."

"It must be admitted," said MacCormack, "that when they put their minds to it, they can be more coriaceous."

"For instance, when they give birth," said Gallager. "We'd make a hell of a fuss if that had to happen to us. Isn't that right, Kelleher?"

"What are you insinuating?"

He'd just circumvented the chin and was coming up the right cheek, having started with the left one. Sweating all over, Larry was keeping quiet. Only his toes were writhing down in the bottom of his socks, but they couldn't be seen.

"We men," said MacCormack, "we belly-ache, when it comes to suffering. But women suffer all the time. You might even say that that's what they're made for."

"You're becoming very gabby," Gallager remarked.

"What *I* say," said Callinan, without looking round, "is to hell with the bloody brutal Sassenachs."

"It's the approach of death that's making him pensive," said Kelleher, who had nearly finished torturing O'Rourke. "You're going to be so handsome," he whispered in the latter's ear.

"We men," MacCormack went on, "when it comes to the fundamental thing . . . you know what I mean . . ."

"And how we know what you mean," said Gallager, pouring the remains of his sauce into the hollow of his hand.

"Well, it's always a pleasure for us. Whereas for women, it's nothing but trouble from the moment they stop being girls . . ."

"Oh I don't know," said Callinan, "there's no need to exaggerate."

"There now, you're superb," said Kelleher, freeing Larry.

The latter sat up and ran his hand over his cheeks: smooth indeed they now were.

"A fine job," said Gallager.

Larry, nevertheless, had little drops of blood all around his face. He gazed dreamily at his crimson palm.

"It's nothing," said Kelleher.

"I'm hungry," said O'Rourke.

MacCormack handed him an opened tin of tuna fish and a bit of bread. But Larry didn't touch them; he held them in his hands, very pensively. Then he stood up and went over towards the little office.

"*She* must be hungry, too," he murmured.

He stopped, and looked round at his companions.

"*I* shall behave correctly towards her."

"What *I* say," said Callinan, "is to hell with the bloody brutal Sassenachs."

"Where on earth can Dillon have got to?" said Kelleher.

"Go and see," said Gallager to O'Rourke.

"*She* mustn't die," said O'Rourke.

"Why not?" said Gallager.

"It wouldn't be fair," said O'Rourke.

"I gave you an order not to talk about her any more."

"She mustn't die," said O'Rourke.

"And what about us?" asked Gallager.

"Go and eat your tuna fish with her, then," said Kelleher. "But maybe she doesn't like men who're too well shaved."

"I love her," said O'Rourke.

"That's enough," said MacCormack.

"I love her," O'Rourke repeated.

His gaze went the rounds of them all, with a far from satisfied expression. They said nothing.

Larry turned on his heel and went over towards the little office.

The bombardment was still in abeyance.

57

CARTWRIGHT read General Maxwell's message once again. The last rebel position must be taken before sundown. They must be able to say that the revolt was at an end, at a complete end. The last rebels were not to be allowed to spend another night.

Cartwright sighed slightly and looked at the Eden Quay post office, merely breached on the first floor. The houses all around it were far more damaged. No more tergiversation was possible. Commodore Cartwright is a traitor neither to his King nor to his Country. And anyway, what was that phantom he'd thought he'd seen? From now on he was going to be bang on target.

He went over to his gunners.

58

LARRY pushed the door shut behind him. He lowered his eyes. He was holding the bread and tuna fish in one hand. Gertie was sitting in an armchair with her back to him. All he could see was her short blond hair.

"I've brought you some light refreshment," said O'Rourke, in a slightly emotional voice.

"Who are you?" Gertie asked harshly.

"My name is Larry O'Rourke, and I'm a medical student."

"You're the one who blew my nose, aren't you?"

Deeply disturbed, Larry mumbled something for a few seconds, and then stopped.

"What have you brought me?"

"Some tuna fish and some bread."

"Put it down there."

Without turning round, she indicated a nearby table. Larry obeyed, and then discovered that the arm that had made the gesture was naked. After which, he perceived the dress spread out over one chair, the slip over another. And he had to come to a conclusion.

He was stunned, shattered, thunderstruck.

"I can hear your breathing," said Gertie, without touching the alimentation.

"My God, my God," murmured O'Rourke, "what have I come here to do?"

"What are you saying?"

"Oh great Saint Joseph, oh great Saint Joseph, I couldn't resist, I couldn't resist, and here I am now, with this woman who seems to me to be in a state of total nudity, and I came to confess my love to her, my chaste, chivalrous and eternal love, but in reality what I want to do is imitate the other swine."

"What are you doing? Are you saying your prayers?"

"I understand myself, now: Callinan and Caffrey, they're my models. Poor girl, poor innocent girl, you've suffered their outrages, yet, deep down, I too want to defile you. Oh Saint Joseph, keep me pure. Oh Saint Mary, couldn't you perform a miracle and give back her virginity to my fiancée Gertrude Girdle?"

"Answer me, for goodness' sake. What are you mumbling?"

"I love you," whispered Larry, in a very, very low voice.

"You're very papist, aren't you?" continued Gertie, who hadn't heard. "But I don't understand why you had to come to me to indulge in your mummery. Are you hoping to convert me?"

"Yes, I am hoping to," replied O'Rourke, in a loud voice. "I can only marry a real Catholic, and you are the girl I want to marry."

Gertie leapt to her feet and turned to face him.

"You're completely crazy," she said harshly. "Don't you realize you're going to die?"

Larry wasn't listening. He could see her now. And not only was she naked, but she was also only wearing a girdle and stockings. O'Rourke gaped.

She stamped her foot:

"Don't you realize that you're going to die? Don't you realize that in a few hours' time you'll be dead? Don't you realize that before the day is out you'll be a corpse?"

"You're beautiful," O'Rourke stammered. "I love you."

"You make me sick, you and your filthy feelings. And anyway, what are those disgusting drops of blood on your cheeks?"

"You are my spouse before God," said O'Rourke.

He raised his eyes to the ceiling, and he all but saw the Eternal Father.

Gertie stamped her foot again:

"Get out! Get out! You nauseate me with your disgusting superstitions."

But Larry was now holding out his arms to her.

"My little wife, my dear little wife."

"Go away. Go away. You're mad."

"May God bless our ideal union."

"Filthy priest, will you kindly leave me alone!"

He took a step towards her.

She retreated.

He took another step towards her.

She retreated another step.

As the room was small, Gertie now found herself with her back to the wall.

Taken from behind, you might say.

Larry kept advancing, with outstretched arms, like someone trying to see through the fog. His fingers made contact with Gertie's skin; he touched her slightly above her breasts. He snatched his hand away, like someone who's burnt himself.

"What am I doing?" he murmured. "What am I doing?"

"Help!" Gertie screamed. "Help! He's a madman!"

59

"DID YOU hear that?" Kelleher asked MacCormack.

MacCormack shrugged his shoulders.

"We ought to have killed her right away, but we had to be correct. And in any case, none of this is very important. Except for the cause. For the cause it's bloody annoying if people are going to be able to say we behaved badly in such tragic moments."

"They'll forgive you," said Kelleher. "It wasn't altogether your fault."

"But who'll know that?" said MacCormack.

"She's got to survive," said Kelleher. "She won't talk. If the British find her corpse amongst ours, that'll look bad. Whereas if she survives, I'm quite sure she'll say we were very decent to her. Which, after all, is true."

"I've got an idea," said MacCormack. "Let's take her down to the cellar. There must be a cellar, here."

"I'll go and look," said Kelleher.

They heard more screams.

"Well well," said Gallager. "I can see I'm going to be the only one that hasn't had her."

"And what about me: d'you think she doesn't interest *me?*" said Kelleher.

Callinan looked round and informed them that things seemed to be stirring once again on the *Furious*.

60

O'ROURKE had grabbed hold of Gertie, but he didn't quite know what to do. She was defending herself, and cursing him. He was pressing her against him, in so far as he could, that is. He'd completely forgotten all he'd been saying a few seconds before. He was simply pondering on the tactics he should adopt, but he no longer realized that he was ratiocinating. He told himself that the best thing would be to throw her on the floor. In the armchair, he couldn't quite see how to go about it.

While he was constructing his plan of attack, he let his hands wander over Gertie's body; since he was pulling her towards him, it was her back that he knew best; and her breasts, because their points were pricking into him. He descended a little lower, and the contact with the elastic tulle seemed to him to be strange, and he considered more than delightful the fact that it covered some substantial attractions.

He was panting, but he still hadn't settled on any decisive method.

Suddenly, she relaxed, and pressed herself up against him. She murmured in his ear (her hair was tickling him in the most delightful fashion):

"You idiot, you think you can . . ."

And yet she seemed agreeable to everything. He even considered her singularly enterprising and audacious, which was strange on the part of a young lady who, after all, with fellows like Callinan and Caffrey, could only have had the most brutal experiences. He decided that this was the moment to kiss her. But Gertie forestalled any unwarranted ulterior familiarities, and demolished his illusions.

He leapt back, howling with pain.

What had hurt him most was not the torsion, but the dirty trick the girl had played on him.

61

"FIRE!"

Thus spake Commodore Cartwright, who was determined to take personal charge of the definitive bombardment.

62

"Buzz," went the shell.

63

THE SHELL traversed the glass roof of the Eden Quay post office and, crashing through the far wall, exploded in the hall. Another shell followed the same trajectory. A third ravaged the first floor. The roof went flying in all directions. Other shells burst on the pavement, and some were still obstinately determined to plough up the Academy garden and mutilate the statues. But most of them made a direct hit on the Eden Quay post office.

After six minutes, Cartwright reckoned they must have achieved some respectable ruins that the General would consider totally satisfactory. He therefore gave the order to cease fire, so that the smoke could clear and they could observe the results. He even considered disembarking, in order to round up the survivors.

64

As soon as things seemed to have quietened down, Mat Dillon came out of the shell-hole in the Academy garden in which he had taken cover. He was pleased to see that the cardboard box he was carrying under his arm had emerged unscathed from this incident.

He had no need of a ladder to get back into the Eden Quay post office, the wall had collapsed, so all he had to do was step over piles of broken bricks. The little door had been blown off. He went into the hall and the first thing he saw was Gertie, on her feet, leaning against a wall, contemplating the disaster with a vague eye. She was no more clad than before. The floor was strewn with corpses. Kelleher, at his machine-gun, was shaking himself and rubbing his head: he had merely been stunned. But MacCormack, Gallager and Callinan all seemed to be well and truly dead. O'Rourke began to groan. He alone had the bad taste to be taking an unconscionable time dying. On the level of their bifurcation, his trousers were stained by a wide, purplish pool. He started calling softly:

"Gertie . . . Gertie . . ."

Dillon put his cardboard box down on a little pile of assorted debris and went over to O'Rourke, who was still groaning:

"Gertie . . . Gertie . . ."

Gertie didn't budge. Dillon observed that Larry had taken too much of a clobbering to be able to survive.

"Courage, old man," he said, "you haven't got much longer."

"Gertie, I love you . . . Gertie, I love you . . . Gertie, I love you . . ."

"Come on, old man, don't talk crap. Would you like me to recite the prayers for the dying?"

"Why doesn't she come over here? Where is she? She's still alive, I know that much."

Dillon raised his head for him and Larry, half-opening his eyes, caught a glimpse of Gertie, still as unclad, still as beautiful. He smiled at her. She looked at him harshly.

"I love you, Gertie. Come over here."

"Oh, come on over," said Mat. "In the state he's in, he won't do you any harm."

"Have you brought me my dress?" she asked him.

"Yes. But do what he asks."

She moved towards them, with a hostile expression. When she was near him, Larry gave her a long look, aesthetically admiring the line of her legs, the curve of her hips, the contour of her breasts. Then he shook his head sadly and shut his eyes again. He stirred slightly, and his hand plunged painfully into his trousers. He brought it out again, bloodstained and closed. Gazing at Gertie, he held it out to her and opened it. She leant over, to get a better look.

"It was for you," he whispered. "It was for you."

His head fell forward, and this time he closed his eyes for good. His arm fell back and the bit of flesh went rolling along the floor. Larry O'Rourke had just died. Dillon laid his head back on the floor, stood up and made the sign of the cross, even though, like every good Catholic, he had a marked tendency towards atheism.

Absent-mindedly, unobtrusively, Gertie kicked the blood-stained little bit of a human being over to the calcinated floorboards, under which it disappeared.

"Poor little thing," she murmured.

She turned to the cardboard box that Mat had put down on the rubble, and grabbed it.

"Is this my dress?" she asked him.

"*Requiescat in pace*," Dillon mumbled. "Between you and me, he must have died in a state of mortal sin."

Dillon sat down on the debris of a chair and meditatively rolled a cigarette. He was examining Gertie with great attention.

"You see," he finally said, "I'd realized that the corset had had its day, but that doesn't mean to say that it won't come back in fashion in one way or another."

"You make me laugh," said Gertie.

"Obviously, you're very beautiful thus begirdled. And not at all hampered in your movements. But . . ."

"You must admit that it's sober, athletic, classic, rational . . ."

"Oh, rational, rational. You don't only need something rational to undress a woman. You see . . ."

Dillon broke off:

"May I call you Gertrude?"

"Oho," said Kelleher who, still riveted to his machine-gun, was listening with all his ears. "Aren't we being polite."

"You see," Mat Dillon went on, "I can well imagine the corset making its reappearance, twenty or thirty years from now."

"What do you suppose I care?"

"I can well imagine an article in a Paris magazine of the time saying something like: 'A revival from a bygone age, the corset makes its sensational come-back at the start of the new season. It will remodel the feminine body, make it into a living statue. These imperatives of fashion will be even more categorical than those of the higher philosophy.' "

"And now he's seized by prophetic inspiration," said Kelleher, who was keeping a watchful eye on the activities of the crew of the *Furious*. "That's what sometimes comes over people, at the hour of death."

"I can see," Dillon went on: " 'half-cup, well-boned, pink nylon brassières. Full breasts repose in them in nests of tulle.' I can see 'wasp-waisted lastex corsets reaching down to the thighs. Their waists are made of a different, stiffer material, which allows the figure to spread out on either side of a tiny waist.' And the article will end by conjuring up memories of the corset which, though it has not been seen since 1916, was nevertheless the great theatrical producer of the new feminine figure: 'ample breasts, wasp waist, and Parisian derrière.' "

"Bravo," said Kelleher, "you talk the most marvelous crap."

"Personally, I prefer my own fashion, because it's what's à la mode today," said Gertie.

"It has a tendency towards masculinity. No buttocks, no breasts, square shoulders."

"It looks as if they're going to disembark," said Kelleher. "They must think we're all dead. I'll let them have another volley, so they can toss us a few more shells."

"I don't know that one," said Gertie, pretending she'd just discovered Kelleher. "Are the others all dead?"

"Starting with Caffrey," Dillon calmly replied.

"Shit!" Kelleher yelled. "Bloody fucking shitting hell! My machine's jammed! And here come those fuckers!"

He started fiddling with his machine-gun.

"Nothing doing. I don't understand."

He turned round to his two surviving companions, and saw Gertie. He hadn't understood a word of her conversation with Dillon, nor the whys and wherefores of the dress. He eyed her up and down with great interest, and walked over to her.

"It's time I put on my dress," she said sweetly.

She put the box down. Dillon cut the string. She opened the box. Dillon unfolded the tissue paper. She looked in the box.

"My wedding dress!" she exclaimed.

And to Dillon:

"How nice of you."

Dillon helped her to put it on.

Kelleher was close by them.

"Get a spurt on. We'll go down to the cellar and shoot at their legs, and then die there heroically. There's no question of their taking us alive."

"No?" Gertie asked him innocently.

"Oh, we'll leave *you* alive. Come on, get a spurt on."

"Where's my brassière? I've lost it."

"It doesn't matter," said Mat, "you don't need one."

"That isn't very correct," said Gertie.

"And you'll keep your trap shut, eh," said Kelleher, "when they find you by our two corpses."

"Keep my trap shut? What does that mean?"

"Come on, Mat, get a spurt on. Anyone might think you were enjoying groping her. Yes, my girl, it means that you've got to keep quiet."

"What about? Why?"

"We're heroes, and not swine. Got it?"

"Perhaps."

"Of course you've got it. If it hadn't been for you we'd have been dead without any trouble, but, just because you went to have a pee at the precise moment of our insurrection, our glory may well be tarnished by vile gossip and filthy slander."

"These things hang by a thread," Dillon absent-mindedly declared.

He retreated a few paces, to contemplate his work of art:

"Beautiful, eh?" he asked Kelleher.

"Yes. She's a peach. You'll end up making me believe that women are tempting creatures."

And to Gertie:

"D'you hear me? Nothing happened. Nothing happened. Nothing happened."

"A man can claim that," Gertie replied, with an immodest smile. "It's different for a woman."

She held his eyes with a severe gaze.

"Or perhaps you don't know? What am I supposed to understand by what you've just said? What does it mean: women may be tempting?"

"That's enough. Now she's all tarted up, let's go underground and face our last fight."

"Come on then," Dillon agreed, philosophically.

Gertie grabbed Kelleher and held him in front of her, without moving.

"Answer me. Don't you realize how idiotic it is, your: 'Nothing happened'? Or must I explain it in sign language?"

"I'm telling you to keep quiet, later, after we're dead."

"What for? For the glory of your Ireland?"

"Yes."

"What a joke," said Gertie.

Dillon intervened:

"Maybe you don't know that she's supposed to be going to marry the fellow who's bombarding us."

"What a joke," said Kelleher.

With an abrupt movement he freed himself from the girl's grasp, and then grabbed her by the arms.

"You're going to keep quiet, aren't you, when we're dead? Caffrey, Callinan, MacCormack, O'Rourke, they were all valiant and pure. You won't desecrate them, eh?"

"If you think I can still remember their names. What's yours?"

"Corny Kelleher," replied Mat Dillon.

"You shut your trap. And why did you provoke us? Our comrades were your victims. You're a whore. What's her name?"

"Miss Gertie Girdle," replied Mat Dillon.

"You're a whore, Gertie Girdle, you're a whore."

"What about your heroic comrades who raped me then, what are they?"

"She's beginning to annoy me," said Kelleher.

"Annoyance is a very feeble feeling," said Gertie.

"Let her go," said Mat. "You'll crease her dress."

"To hell with her dress. I want her to promise us to keep quiet."

"You said yourself that she'd never dare, that those aren't the sort of things a young fiancée could say . . ."

"That remains to be seen," said Gertie.

"I see the situation a bit better, now," Kelleher declared.

"It's obvious," said Gertie. "You're crushed. You're going to die."

"That's not the point. The point is you. You haven't seen enough yet."

"What d'you want her to see?" asked Dillon.

Gertie threw herself against Kelleher, laughing.

"What next?" she said. "What next?"

She glued her mouth to his, and forced a passage between his teeth.

He began to caress her breasts, and felt their nipples becoming erect.

"She hasn't seen enough yet," he repeated, with somber obstination. "She *must* keep quiet. She hasn't seen enough yet."

Mat Dillon rolled another cigarette and watched what was going on with curiosity. The situation was becoming singularly animated.

"They're going to ruin my dress," he murmured.

Then the situation was reversed, and Mat began to understand Kelleher's intentions. He didn't know whether he ought to approve of them, but now, in the middle of this disaster, within a few hours, certainly no more, or even perhaps a few minutes, of death, it was really all the same to him, and

RAYMOND QUENEAU

anyway, his feelings for Kelleher were always of the greatest tenderness, the greatest indulgence.

"Hold her," Kelleher told him.

It was indeed what he had guessed. He flicked his cigarette away, grabbed Gertie with a vigor she hadn't thought him capable of, and held her still. She was quite willing, in any case, because *she* hadn't yet understood.

"But," she soon exclaimed, "you mustn't do that. But you don't know how to go about it. But I assure you, that's not the way to do it with a woman. But you're just an ignorant brute. You think you're doing it with another gentleman. But I tell you it isn't like that. But I don't want to. But I don't want to. But . . . But . . ."

"The bugger!" yelled Kelleher. "Now she won't say anything, she won't say anything, and no one will be able to say we weren't heroes, valiant, pure heroes. Finnegans wake!"

"Finnegans wake!" replied Dillon, who was filled with emotion by everything that was happening. "I wouldn't mind making her keep quiet, too," he suggested timidly.

Changing hands, Gertie continued to dispute the fundamental merits of the case.

65

THERE is one quality that no one can deny the British, and that is tact. The sailors from the *Furious* had disembarked near the Eden Quay post office and entered it unobtrusively, some armed with rifles and others with grenades. They had encircled the group of survivors, who were oblivious of their surroundings, but they waited to intervene until everything was over, for the last thing they wished was to see the young lady blush in their presence, thinking they might have surprised her in an immodest position.

So her dress fell down over her feet again; she straightened up, her face very red and very moist with tears; Kelleher and Dillon looked at each other in triumph; whereupon they felt the point of a bayonet pricking their backs. They put their hands up.

66

COMMODORE CARTWRIGHT, accompanied by his lieutenants, set foot on land. At the risk of getting their shoes dusty, they penetrated into the ruins of the Eden Quay post office. The sailors had already laid the corpses down in a corner, in order of height. Two other rebels, standing against the remains of a wall, were waiting, with raised arms.

Cartwright perceived Gertie, who threw herself into his arms.

"Darleeng, darleeng," she whispered.

"My dearest, my dearest," he replied.

The only thing that surprised him a little was that, in such circumstances, she should be wearing a wedding dress. But, no less tactful than his sailors, he didn't mention it.

"Excuse me," he said, "but I still have some duties to fulfill. We must pass judgment on these two rebels. Naturally, in their capacity as rebels captured in possession of firearms, we shall condemn them to death, isn't that right, gentlemen?"

Teddy Mountcatten and the first officer considered the matter for a few moments, and then agreed.

"My dearest, forgive me asking you such a question, but these rebels, did they . . . how shall I put it . . . did they behave correctly towards you?"

Gertie looked at Dillon, Kelleher and then the corpses.

"No," she said.

Cartwright paled. Kelleher and Dillon remained impassive.

"No," said Gertie. "They tried to lift up my beautiful white dress to look at my ankles."

"The swine," grunted Cartwright. "That's the Republicans all over, filthy lascivious beasts."

"Forgive them, darleeng," miaowed Gertie. "Forgive them."

"Impossible, my dearest. In any case, they have already been condemned to death, and we are going to execute them forthwith, as the law requires."

He went over to them.

"Did you hear? The military tribunal, over which I preside, has condemned you to death, and you are going to be executed forthwith. Say your last prayers. Sailors, prepare for action."

The firing squad got into position.

"I wish to add that, contrary to what you believe, you do not deserve a worthy place in the chapter of World History devoted to heroes. You have dishonored yourselves by the base gesture that my fiancée, her legitimate modesty notwithstanding, had no choice but to describe. Are you not ashamed of having tried to lift up a young lady's dress in order to admire her ankles? Lecherous characters, you will die like dogs, with a tarnished, despairing conscience."

Kelleher and Dillon trembled not a whit. Behind Cartwright's back, Gertie stuck her tongue out at them.

"What have you to say for yourselves?" Cartwright demanded.

"We always treat women too well," said Kelleher.

"How true," sighed Dillon.

A few seconds later, peppered with bullets, they were dead.

ABOUT THE TYPE

The text of this book has been set in Trump Mediaeval. Designed by Georg Trump for the Weber foundry in the late 1950s, this typeface is a modern rethinking of the Garalde Oldstyle types (often associated with Claude Garamond) that have long been popular with printers and book designers.

Trump Mediaeval is a trademark of
Linotype-Hell AG and/or its subsidiaries

TITLES IN SERIES